A Glass of Water

OTHER TITLES BY JIMMY SANTIAGO BACA
PUBLISHED BY GROVE PRESS

Memoir:
A Place to Stand

Poetry:
Healing Earthquakes
C-Train and Thirteen Mexicans

Fiction:
The Importance of a Piece of Paper

JIMMY
SANTIAGO
BACA

A Glass of Water

Grove Press
New York

Published simultaneously in Canada
Printed in the United States of America

FIRST EDITION

ISBN-13: 978-0-8021-1922-3

Grove Press
an imprint of Grove/Atlantic, Inc.
841 Broadway
New York, NY 10003

Distributed by Publishers Group West

www.groveatlantic.com

09 10 11 12 13   10 9 8 7 6 5 4 3 2 1

For my kids Esai and Lucia—but especially for my love, Stacy, who helped me while I wrote this book, helped me emotionally and spiritually and made the time for me to write. Also, to my friend Marcos, who worked in the fields in Yuma and gave me the title for the novel, who told me a glass of water is the most important thing to a field-worker. Thank you.

A Glass of Water

Part One

1

Everyone is gathered in the camp compound around a bonfire to drink and eat and remember my life. I feel their boots above me shifting dirt, the air groan with the aroma of barbecued goat. I hear the field-workers blow their noses, cough, and spit out leaf dust, and as the afternoon wears on a dozen or so get drunk and weep over memories of me on stage and how I expressed their sorrow or joy in my songs. Others start fistfights because their memories of my singing scorches their reason. The quiet, humble ones pass out on the dirt.

In each heart, to every one of them, I remain a green-feathered parrot in a golden cage of memory, but when I was living each day was a smattering of eggshell fragments smeared with predator's saliva. La Muerte, or Death, prowled the margins of my days, peering out from bounty hunter eyes, INS patrols, vigilante groups, and ICE and border patrol agents.

But I was determined to dance for my oppressed people, my heart urged and so I did. I was an eagle, hatched to fly where I wanted, a woman on a journey who arrived a thousand times to blunt the blade of cruelty, to scald her eyes with anger's fire because she could not accept the sorrow of life, was unprepared to hear children's voices in the soft evening breeze speak of slaughters carried out by soldiers along the New Mexico border.

Now, as I listen to the mourners, lowering their eyes as they mention my name, smelling of beer, cigarette smoke, and sweat, truck *keys jangling from rings at their belt loops, I realize they knew me quite well.*

I want to tell them something but I have seeped in under alley stones and dirt to blood's birthplace, and my language is the molten core where fire and matter merge to create the music of minerals that become earth, and if you look at the hills and mountains and fields, you gaze at me, I am near you, next to you, beneath, above, and beside you.

I hear one man saying, "She was a better singer than Chavela, Lola Beltrán, or Amalia Mendoza but things don't work out sometimes; why a man would cut her throat, silence her—dear, dear God."

2

Thirst was on me my first step in the field, it churned in my stomach, cried in every muscle, demanding water. Thirst was master.

I sometimes hallucinated leaf dew was a gourd of water—my fingers, shoulders, and neck lost their aching and time seemed to get lost somewhere, to float around and around over the fields like a bird that had nothing to do as sweat dripped down my back and brow, and everything seemed to loft in the air when the illusions came. You couldn't hear anything, couldn't taste anything, couldn't see anything, and you had no clue where you were; you were put in a place where no one else was, you were all alone and you were happy and pleased and you finally thought you had reached the paradise you had been working for all these days, working all your life for this place and it finally came to you in this muddy field with fleas and flies and wasps and all sorts of flying bugs biting and itching at you. Here it came, landing on your drenched T-shirt and shading your eyes for a moment, an eternal moment, and whisking you off. Every nerve had a calmness you never experienced, you had never even realized such peace existed because no one had ever told you about it, no book or Bible ever preached a place like this that came to you when you were at your lowest ebb and you couldn't take anymore and you couldn't believe in anything else.

I knew it wasn't real but I couldn't help but look and stare and lick my lips at the mirage fading into shimmering heat waves and I'd keep on bending and picking as thirst nested under my tongue, becoming a deep hungering darkness that ground itself into my bones and brain and gave me no rest or mercy, a thirst that made me believe I was the worst-off human being in the world. That kind of thirst, that kind of despair came over me and never let me go. I became its prisoner and I belonged to it forever. It owned every part of my life, it claimed me completely.

And that was how I lived. I worked my life around it, made my dreams around thirst, decided on plans around thirst, always kept it in front of my eyes and in my mind. I never once got up and didn't have to think about thirst, never once did I look out over the horizon or at the sky and not think about thirst, and no matter how many glasses of water I gulped down, it seemed to grow and it became larger and wanting more, always wanting more.

But when that man cut my throat I never had a thirst so fierce, a thirst for life as mine was being drained. I would have drunk urine or vomit at that moment, my mouth contorting for one more drop of life, death inching and edging its way on me, shriveling in every pore and sucking my soul out, my raspy throat stinging like bees maddened by a poker, my tongue swelling, my lungs suffocating. And through clenched teeth, as I begged for one more second, I quenched myself on memories of my two boys back in the bar crawling around the floor under tables, me doing my sound check on the stage mic, gasping through my tears and blood, worried my baby boys might be sitting on the floor biting into a pebble as if it was candy or catching hands under dresses, and my beautiful husband waiting on me to return. I tell you, never a thirst so fierce as wanting one more second of life with my family.

3

January 2006

Casimiro was burning brush and tumbleweeds. The night sky twinkled with stars and the red-hot moon was slowly fading. He raked and scooped up embers in his shovel, glanced at his watch— it was a little after 5:00 a.m. He stepped near the heat and the crackle of the flames pleased him. Within the hour he finished scorching the northeast corner of one field and started banking smoky mounds of burning ash.

He privately begrudged God for allowing Nopal to have been butchered so savagely. She deserved better than that. He knew the proper way of enduring Nopal's absence was through prayer but it didn't do much to alleviate his chronic melancholy. His Catholic faith offered little relief and the only way to tolerate her absence was working dawn to dusk.

His stomach churned with the memory of the crime he had committed in Mexico. It was a curse that followed him, trailed his footsteps to America like a black scorpion in the dirt, a white one under the sheets, a clear one in the water basin he washed his face in every morning, a red and green one in the rows of chili he worked, and a golden one in the blistering sun on his brow, the poison of its many stings settling in his empty heart.

The last Saturday afternoon of her life they'd varnished the floor and stained the paneling in the Pullman car they called home, Nopal humming his favorite Mexican *corrido,* which she had written about his coming to America when he was sixteen.

In September 1983, in the village of Villa de Alonzo, Casimiro was given the gruesome task of pitching corpses onto carts and hauling them down to the crematorium. The village had almost been wiped out from some kind of strange virus. The work done, he put his torch to the roof timber of homes and as the flames devoured houses they shredded every aspect of his identity, reduced his previous life to a meaningless mound of smoldering ash. And it was an obvious sign: God's message was to start his life anew, and so, invigorated with a renewed faith that better things lay beyond the horizon, he bid the remaining inhabitants adios and left.

But that was not the only reason he left.

He remembered his father saying, "Sometimes a man is so poor, all the pride he has is in the last cigarette he's smoking." And it was true. A day or so into the trip he sat on a boulder and smoked his last cigarette, feeling a little pride that he had escaped, inventing a story in his mind in case he needed to explain himself to authorities, a story to replace the real one left back in Mexico.

And though he had tried to bury the incident in the ashes with the houses in his village, each dawn the pistol and the man's expression when he shot him charred his mind and heart, and he could sniff the air every day and smell it, breathe it into his lungs. The crime was his burden to carry in life, carry alone until he died, keep it close to his heart and tell no one lest his two sons inherit the affliction.

He sensed, however, that the curse had already taken what he loved most in life, his wife, Nopal.

He coughed now as the field smoke blew his way. "What do you think, *pájaros*? It was my fault, is it not so?" he asked the sparrows skimming the blackened field, referring to the fact that he had saved Nopal that day, married her and had children with her, only to have her taken from him.

The sun was coming up. He resumed tending the burn line. He appeared dreamlike—an aging, five foot six silhouette against a horizon blushed with daybreak, a shadow wearing a dirt-stained baseball cap to shade his eyes from the smoke, denim collar up around his neck and ears, waistline riding high, and khaki trouser cuffs stuffed into his oversize boots, red bandanna over his nose and mouth to keep from breathing the smoke. The bandanna was the one Nopal used to wear in her hair.

The breeze spiraled smoke as he sifted dirt over a flash fire, dousing flash points as they materialized. Now and then he blew on a twig to get a flame, carrying it lit to redirect and control the fire line's widening circle.

Nearby, prairie dogs and black-footed ferrets bolted across his line of vision, panicked quails chirped excitedly, rattlesnakes melted, scorpions and tarantulas squirmed to cinders, and coyotes howled beyond in the semidark.

He heard a hiss, a squeal, and a *rack-tack* sound which he believed was a spirit, humoring itself at his expense. He watched as the spirit twitched its windy tail, teasing smoke to flurry around him and knock his hat off, gusting ember clouds and ash dust that choked him, and he jaunted off, slapping his chest.

He took a water bottle from his coat pocket and gulped, snorting phlegm out through his nostrils and spitting until his saliva was clean and he could swallow.

He watched the wind spirit skim ground as weeds huffed up and danced back and forth on the breeze. After a bit he worked the charred ground again, shoveling dirt to douse small fires that had rekindled over the boundaries, and watched as hundreds of tiny flames flashed then dwindled.

He was thirty-nine. He had been in America twenty-three years but it seemed like he had arrived only yesterday. Leaning on his shovel, mesmerized by hundreds of lit embers, he retreated into memory.

I am standing in the desert, looking around, expecting something to happen, it is very strange and confusing to me.

I walk most of the time at night but I decide to walk even though it is daytime. Soon I see an object in the distance. I turn in its direction, thinking hopefully there might even be a person and it would be refreshing because it has been weeks since I talked, except to myself, to the coyotes and lizards I see along the way, or to God when I pray.

I hurry to reach it so I can rest under some shade—the heat is unbearable but I vow to get in another ten miles after a brief siesta. What is it, out in the middle of nowhere? A plane crash? An old miner's shack? Maybe God will tell me the purpose of sparing me. Maybe God will work His will through me.

I am finally in front of a truck. I smell the foulest odor I have ever smelled and I want to get as far away from it and keep running until I turn back and see nothing but open desert.

I call out for God to help me and I hear a single little voice and I think it's my imagination. God's voice sounds strange. I hear it again, weaker.

I say out loud, "Now, is this really happening, are you people really people? Can you hear me, are you really there? I am here and the sun is above and the air is still and I walked here a little while ago."

I take a rock, break the lock, and push the big door, and as it goes back sunlight floods the dark space. There is chicken wire blocking access into the back part of the truck. I try to move it, handling it roughly, and swing the screen away. There is another barricade of plywood and cardboard siding. I shove the barrier aside and the smell is unbearable.

I fall to my knees, praying as fast as I can for God to know that I was not involved in this crime. I weep. I want the poor victims to know I am here. I want them to hear me and my crying grows louder into groaning and through my tears and groans I shout prayers, yelling words like a madman, turning around on my knees in circles, until the voice comes again.

It takes away my breath. I am lightheaded and am going to fall over, feeling I might pass out, thinking I am lost in another kind of reality and, looking around, I beg the angels to protect my soul.

I hear the voice, a woman's voice.

My mind has gone blank and I can't think of what to do because it is so overwhelming. Maybe I got hit over the head, maybe I am having a nightmare. I am really asleep and I need to wake up and get on the road but I'm too exhausted to raise myself.

I can't come up with an answer and it scares me and I try to tell myself not to be scared, that there is an answer for everything that happens. I am trying to move, trying to speak, trying to do something, to move an inch with my feet or raise my arm, maybe, to motion in the air, but I can't do anything.

I pray to God to help me decide what to do next and little by little I start to move. First my feet and hands, then I turn my head and see bodies tangled on top of bodies twisted and bloated, piles of rotting bodies, all tied together with rope, shirts crawling with maggots, drenched in slimy intestines, mucus, and body fluids, straw hats, neck medals, and rosaries still clutched by dead fingers, gunnysack belongings strapped on backs infested with flies and insects.

My body has seized up, petrified where I am standing, but in a panic, with great effort, I slowly pry one foot up, then step forward until I grip the ledge of the truck bed, squinting intently at the dark in the back, searching for God's voice and I find her.

4

February 1984

He found her—thin, hair falling out, shoulder bones and ribs
gaunt. For the first two weeks he had to help her walk and eat.
She quivered and trembled but eventually she put on weight and
regained her vitality. She was a stunning woman.

They cut prairie grass to sleep on alongside the Rio Grande
under cottonwoods and willows, shared the fish and rabbits they
caught with others going north—Juanito, to Iowa to the Tyson
chicken factory; Benito, to California wine country; Maria, to
North Carolina tobacco and soy fields; Chaco, to New York to
wait tables, cook, and wash dishes.

They had been traveling slowly but surely north when one
afternoon, against the horizon, a huge, monstrous snarling machine came at them. It grunted, magnifying in growling size as it
neared, guttering dust, diesel oil, and exhaust smoke. They froze.

It was going to run them over, tires almost on them, when
suddenly the driver geared down and the earthmover coughed
soot as it crunched to a stop. They were dwarfed by the tires the
height of a two-story house and because they had heard no man-
made sounds for so long the machine's idling, shaking the earth
beneath their feet, was all the more terrifying.

A man in goggles leaned out of the cab and yelled, "What're you doing out here?" He sized them up, then instructed, "Keep walking that way, you'll run into my place. Wait for me."

The man shifted gears and drove off with a ponderous explosion of dirt that settled for minutes in its wake. The engine roared the air until it vanished and then, as they walked, waves of silence hummed over them.

Late that afternoon Miller hired them on a temporary basis to cut the weeds around his house, weeds so tall a horse could stand in them and not be seen by an observer.

Casimiro was resourceful and Nopal ingenious as they renovated Miller's place. They tacked on roof shingles, installed a sturdy wraparound porch railing, planted apple and pear trees, yanked out old piñon posts and dug new holes, stretched a mile of good fencing, finished off his garage, welded an entrance gate, and laid stone along the edge of the blacktop driveway leading up to Miller's imported English front door, which was embossed with a coat of arms and family initials.

The day Casimiro and Nopal showed up, Miller had fired four Anglos who, combined, couldn't do the work of one Nopal. The couple did the work of five good men and Miller paid them what only one would charge. He was impressed and kept them on.

He showed Casimiro how to run the backhoe and taught Nopal the basics on a Ditch Witch, and while Casimiro excavated a main canal from the Rio Grande to irrigate the chili fields they would one day cultivate, Nopal trenched ditches that would feed the rows. They worked from 5:00 a.m. to midnight for three months and by the end of May they had cleared, disked, and leveled fifty acres running parallel to Interstate I-25.

One evening, under a full moon, Casimiro and Nopal went up to the interstate in the tractor and stood on the road shoulder. They faced west and could see the whole lay of the land. Below them to the right was Miller's place, a two-story imitation English country mansion with a hodgepodge of Moorish features—a red tile roof, porch arches, and a series of somber windows and doors facing the road. It was white with green trim.

A mile beyond his house, fields unfolded in an uninterrupted fairy tale and at the north end of the fifty acres was a Pullman railcar set on bricks, field machinery, and various building structures. As far as the eye could follow ran a continuous background of cottonwoods concealing the Rio Grande, a wall of leaves so dense that midday air was blue under its canopy.

Behind them, sixteen-wheelers zoomed by toward Las Cruces and El Paso but it didn't cheapen the romance of the moment or the exhilarating sense they felt that they could do anything they wanted in this life as long as they were together.

He was sixteen, she fifteen. They were feeling how much they had accomplished as their eyes slowly moved south to north along the graded rows, perfect and straight, not a single weed or break in the mounds as water poured from the main canal, row on row, glimmering in the furrows, and they knew it was time to move on to a big city and maybe start a family.

They kissed.

The next day, however, to persuade them to remain indefinitely, Miller gave them each a fifty dollar bonus, plus a dollar an hour raise for Casimiro and promoted him to supervisor over future Mexican workers. He drove them in his used air-conditioned truck along the Rio Grande, across open meadows and, finally, into a clearing where he promised, if they stayed, some day he'd sell them this part of the land, around twenty acres. He'd give them the old Pullman railcar to fix up and live in, and concluded, "If you decide to stay and help me make this into a real agricultural business, I'll throw this pickup in, too."

Casimiro knew that even though it was old enough for the license plate numbers to be unreadable, it ran well. The following day he wasted no time putting the truck to use. He went to Las Cruces, picked up the lumber and rafters Miller had ordered, and hired a dozen migrants.

Over the next few months, Casimiro and his new crew erected a huge barn, a packing shed, a storage warehouse, and six open-air lean-to sheds to park farm equipment under.

Nopal was pregnant and they were here to stay.

5

When you wish to talk to me, Lorenzo, feel me, I live in your lower back, my son, in the muscles used for bending and rising. I am a heavy clay bowl in your stomach in which to pour your fear. Your spine is a canyon trail I walk and I am the latch handle you turn in the dark to let light enter.

When I left you, all you had was my name, hugging it with your lips, my name shattering the silence of your sorrow, savoring it on your tongue because you thought I was going to return, flying through the night like an angel to sweep you up in my arms but I was taken away forever and became more a presence to you in death than in life—five years old, for months in the fields, no taller than a chili plant, your head low, eyes on your hands, raising your voice higher and higher, you repeated my name until you became lost in the quivering sound, the sound of Mama, Mama, falling into the sound of my name, that soaked up your sadness at my absence.

After what happened to me there was nothing else, no consolation, no thought or hope to make it disappear. Even the warm buttered tortilla tasted bitter, it was complete defeat, the flame of your small gray-haired soul dimmed to a weak flicker and then an ember in the dark.

You had to reshape how you saw yourself in the world, redefine your meaning, create new understandings of how to live without me. Every second of every day your joy blurred, eyes that had given you sight to *pull things in were ablaze with the white blindness of grief. The reason to see connections in life was extinguished and the lonely nights rattled their raspy death seeds in your hands after I departed.*

You repeated my name a million times to undo what had happened. Looking over the plants, across furrows, beyond the backs and bent heads of field workers, you still believe sometimes you see me coming down the rows with my basket to join you.

My oldest, I gave you my guitar. It's good you burned my songs: a son can't take his mother's recipes acquired during a lifetime and get the same taste and flavor. Her soul is in them and it's dangerous to take the moon-part of the person, a little of which went into every teaspoon and measuring-cupful note.

You didn't know how to distribute the light each word carries, how to illuminate one word more than another, how to let a word cool in the shade of one's purring, another to purge rage in throaty snarls, or simmer a jazzy soup out of words lifted up from the never-healed wounds.

My true gift to you, sweet son, was to teach you to see through the eyes of a woman's heart.

6

April 2002

Saturday morning, on the road before daybreak. It was Lorenzo's eighteenth birthday and to celebrate he was aiming to stack up steak-and-potato money at the jackpot rodeo—cowboys pay up their entrance fee and whoever comes up on top takes home the winnings. During the spring he got in as many weekend jackpot rodeos as he could, traveling the circuit from Silver City to Socorro, Belen, Los Lunas, Moriarty, Watrous, Willard, Las Vegas, Tucumcari, Española, Tierra Amarilla, Questa, and Raton.

After driving a little over two hours across the prairie, he pulled into Willard's hot, dusty rodeo grounds, a poor boy's raunchy sage and tumbleweed meadow lined with beat-up ranch trucks and rusting stock trailers, horses tied to the shady side with a bucket of water. He wasn't there for roping, he was there for an entirely different game: bronc riding.

He knew most of the riders, a unique breed of rough stock cowboys, not raised on daddy's lap in new air-conditioned tractors. Most couldn't afford to keep horses, they were horse-poor, all guts, willing to risk everything for a shot at the nationals and, God willing, with enough heart and luck, to make it to the big money.

He pulled his truck around to the area where the bronc riders parked apart from the others, slowly driving by cowboys who slept in their trucks, some of whom were standing around yawning, stretching cramped legs, others who were rubbing wax and yanking on bronc cinches and hand ropes with serious faces. No fancy felt cowboy hats and pressed shirts—they were spitting, crease-faced, scuffed, and weathered as old leather, dreaming of escape from the poverty they'd been born into.

Their eyes peered out from their reassembled facial bones, the kicked-in cheeks, broken jaws, split lips, and smashed noses. One-meal-a-day eaters, taking care of what they had because the leather got better the older it was—worn to fit them—like clubhouse boxers who got trampled and beat down for a living, sometimes killed.

With used-up lives, pain staining the innocent texture of their smiles, reared with more guidance by a horse than an adult, birthdays and holidays celebrated in a dirt corral with a horse and sardines and crackers, changing clothes in truck stops, just-getting-by ones, trying-to-do-right ones, I-don't-care-anymore ones.

7

He drew a bronc named Cocaine. A rodeo hand herded the other broncs into a separate corral and secured them, leaving Cocaine alone—he was a black-gray dappled bronc, snorting and kicking his rear legs high in the air at anyone that came near, banging his head against the fence siding wildly.

Lorenzo bought a piece of cold watermelon from an old lady selling food out of a Styrofoam ice chest and squeezed through the crowd of onlookers, gnawing the melon as he appraised the bronc. Cocaine caught his look, threw his head in the air, sauntered, twirled, and kicked the fencing where Lorenzo stood. The crowd shuffled back, murmuring that the horse was crazy.

"You bastard," he whispered and threw the watermelon rind at the bronc and Cocaine bucked and rocked the railings; their eyes locked and Cocaine lurched at him with such hatred he dented the side rails of the pen. An old cowboy pulled the handle and flung the gate open, then dashed for safety as Cocaine blasted out into the corral with the rest of the broncs, every nerve crackling like a windblown prairie flame.

That evening, for eight ruthless seconds, Lorenzo was astride an exploding star—Cocaine, with his spittle-drooling nostrils, huffing foam, every slingshot muscle discharging eruptions with every buck—and for eight seconds, Lorenzo was pitched through infinity, curving above the earth, spinning past planets, flipping over and falling for what seemed forever until he hit ground, landing on his right shoulder.

8

The next morning he collected his winnings, filled up his 66 Chevy truck in the town of T or C, and on the interstate rolled his window down. He inhaled, tasting the moist air from Elephant Butte Reservoir. Heading south on I-25, he opened the brown paper bag he had bought from local high school girls raising money for 4-H, unwrapped the green chili and potato burrito, and practically swallowed it whole it was so good, then poured himself a cup of black coffee from his thermos and leaned back and cruised. It was the kind of morning that touched his heart with joy—the bluest sky, the headiest sage scents, home-cooked food, a good running motor, the land's mysterious beauty words could never describe—it didn't get any better than this.

When he topped the last hill he saw Miller's place. His mother had told him how it used to be a shack in a once barren land, and Miller's place anything but a castle. But now, more than fifteen years later, white pipe fence encircled the impeccably pruned orchards and landscaped rose gardens, in the middle of which black and white swans floated in the pond that Vito and Jose had made, and spread out beside it was the golf course built with his father's supervision and Mexican labor.

His eyes rested on the small adobe patched with landfill scraps—*la cantina* his mother had sung in, now owned by Arabs.

His child's heart memory of the man's black scuffed boots entering *la cantina* had never left. The boots paused within a foot of him under a table. And he noticed the boot tips and heels plated with buffalo nickels. And for some crazy reason those buffalo nickels had gouged a rut in his heart and the image of them had remained prominent in his memory of the long-ago evening that still filled his lungs with dread. When the memory came to him, as it often did, it consumed his attention as a specter slowly appearing, as if he were dreaming with his eyes open.

He'd been so proud of himself, carrying a cigar box full of treasures—candies, a rubber play knife, Mexican coins, a broken rosary, a yo-yo missing string, a shaving brush with no bristles, plastic Indians and soldiers. He had clutched the box as he followed the dirt road to *la cantina* and found his mother doing sound checks on the stage mic, his eyes dazzled by the string of red and green lights surrounding the stage.

He stashed his cigar box behind the bar on top of the crate of whiskey bottles and went looking for his little brother, crawling around under tables and roaming along baseboards looking for coins. At the tables, beneath vinyl booths, cowboy boots and work boots reeked of manure and fertilizer chemicals. Lorenzo pocketed pennies, cigarette butts, nail clippers, and black combs.

His mother was the center of the world here and he could feel the excitement. Above him barmaids lit table candles in Coke cans perforated with holes. He peeked out from under a table, listening as Amado, the owner, always with bloodshot eyes, greeted people. "*Oye Juan—qué tal Maria—y pues Jose—andale Francisco,* enter, enter."

And as the night wore on and people sat, rapt, listening to his mother sing, he remembered the exact moment the man entered, distinctly recalled the smell, sounds, and sights of the cantina and the man wearing black boots with heels and tips plated in buffalo nickels. He sensed the man had ill intentions toward his mother.

Amid standing applause and whistles, he looked up at the man staring at his mother and felt an ice pick puncture his five-year-old heart. That evening, on the way home with his mother and brother, it rained heavily, brimming arroyos, and in the splattered windshield, as the wipers swiped back and forth, he saw the man's face and its features chilled him with goosebumps.

9

He took exit 81 west, followed the ramp to his right into the valley, passed the now empty roadside stalls that sold chili, garlic, squash, watermelons, pinto beans, tortillas, and tamales, and drove until he turned onto the north-south dirt road leading to camp.

On wide paths running east-west between the fields, big flatbed wagons were hitched to tractors ready to be filled and towed to the packing sheds. Alongside were more than thirty cars and pickups with hoes, knives, water coolers, and lunch buckets stuffed with hot sodas and cold burritos; when workers stopped for lunch, that's what it was—hot sodas and cold burritos and they loved it.

When he pulled in, women were spraying plastic pesticide tanks, next to the packing sheds, dogs and children splashing in the pools of wastewater.

Carmen, a college girl, here at the camp for only five weeks, doing research for her thesis on migrants, came out wearing a packer's plastic green apron and rubber gloves. "Did you win?" He threw her a thumbs-up and asked her to tag along while he checked on the field-workers.

"I've been thinking," she began, "how they just sent Vito away." She set her apron and gloves on an oil drum. "That's so unjust!"

"Why?"

"Did he have a hearing? Is there an appeal process? Just because it was the boss's jackass son."

"He's judge and jury here, he hires and fires."

"It's bullshit."

"Maybe, but it's the way it is. One phone call and we're in jail or deported. He calls *la migra* and they'll dump us all on the border like a bunch of dogs. You got some learning to do."

"They can't do that to you, you were born here."

"They can deport my dad and all the others."

They walked in silence to a far field where the migrants were picking in force.

"What's going on over there?" She indicated heavy equipment and construction going on beyond the fields in the distance.

"We flooded last year, washed out trailers and roads, the waters closed down or knocked down schools, homes, you name it. Scared them so bad many of the migrants sold their tiny lots to Miller. He's building condos, gated homes. River land is prime real estate."

They passed women picking in the rows, lip syncing while listening to their iPods. Carmen heard a big heavy black woman call to a Chicana in the next row, "Isabel, you going to the bar tonight?"

The middle-aged Chicana said, "If Ruben's there."

"Get off that Ruben, baby. You too pretty and young to waste your time with a man who don't appreciate the finer aspects of your beauty."

"Retha, once you got him in your bones, you got him in your bones."

Carmen and Lorenzo walked a good two miles, past the fields, all the way to the open-air stalls. They sat on a picnic bench and drank cold watermelon juice.

"Why aren't these kids in school," Carmen asked, looking at the teenage cooks and servers working the stalls.

"They were until the mothers found out the school put them all in one room and made them just sit there all day. They got no books, no teaching, nothing. Day after day they just sat there, talked to each other from nine to three in the afternoon."

"That's illegal, they can't do that."

"There's laws for you, then there's laws for us."

"Believe me, in San Diego there are plenty of Mexicans doing a lot better than you and me. They get Medicare, welfare, food stamps, schools are packed with them. My mom and dad are middle-class Hispanics and they worked so hard to get ahead—and I work so fricken hard to get ahead—and you know when my mom got pneumonia she couldn't get into the hospital because all the beds were taken by Mexicans, and the way they look at you, they act like they're so much better."

"If you hate them so much why are you here?"

"I don't hate them, I'm just saying I don't pity them—and I don't have to tell you, especially you, that there are two kinds of Mexicans: these, and those in the cities who exploit the system."

And just then, as though to prove her point, a group of Mexican teenagers drove in and piled out of a new Jeep Cherokee. The girls flaunted glossy black and red high heels, sleek designer cowgirl jeans that revealed their panty thongs, which their boyfriends, in jeans and T-shirts, kept pulling on. When they sat down to eat Carmen noticed that all the teenagers from the Cherokee had tattoos—a blue eagle, a black mustang, an Irish flag, a green heart.

Two Mexicans pulled up behind the Cherokee in an old beat-up Camaro and didn't say a word between them as they ate *caldo* and *menudo* to soothe their hangovers. Lorenzo could smell the starch in their clean clothes, their strong cologne.

"Immigrants fresh over the border looking for work," Lorenzo said. "The leaf blower in the backseat is for appearance in case *la migra* stops them. Come on, I need to get some work done."

They started to walk back. "Here's some more information for your college paper. You notice most Mexicans carry a salt shaker on their belt instead of a knife? They love watermelon."

"You joking?"

"Nope."

After a while she asked, "What do you do for fun out here?"

"On weekends I play poker, go fishing, get a haircut in town. Work on my truck."

"That doesn't sound like much fun to me."

"Most work on weekends to fill up the next tank of gas so they can keep moving north to better jobs."

They arrived at the Pullman, his dad's place, and sat down at a table outside under an elm tree. Carmen ran over to the warehouse and came back a few minutes later.

"Go on." She turned on a hand-size recorder and held it in her palm to record what he was saying. "It's okay to be a little nervous . . . take your time."

"I was just thinking how my mom would send me and Vito ahead of her to pick the loose chilies. We'd stack them in piles in the furrow row and we'd wait for her at the end of the row and she'd come behind us scooping up the piles, filling her sack. When she got to us we'd curl up on the gunnysack and go to sleep."

"They make sacks that big?" she asked.

"We each got one and she sewed ours to hers. Tied a rope to the top and looped the other end around her waist and while she picked, she dragged us. She'd pause to strip the chili plants—pull, pause, pull, pause. I spent the first five years as a baby inhaling the smell of pepper leaves and soil, rocked by mother's rhythms and the sound of women talking across rows.

"I remember certain times the heat got someone and he'd holler God was telling him something. And if it wasn't the sun burning their brains, it was the moon calling to their hearts—a lot of kids were conceived at night between those chili rows. Lots of loving in those fields girl, lots of loving."

10

Here, playing barefoot in God's breath, I forget about myself. Here, memories surface like a harvest of frogs in the rain.

One is my youngest son, Vito, and if you didn't know him, he could chafe your patience like steel bristles on a sunburned scalp. You wouldn't know he is considerate, with a relish for life, that goodness glows from him, that everyone loves the openness of this giant kid, huge for seventeen, a towering six foot three.

It isn't your broad nostrils that inhale the fragrance of dawn, radiator steam, and hot bald tires that one first notices; not your mischievous smile showcasing ivory teeth, or lips shapely as maguey leaves, or your Tarahumara cheeks and Apache jaw. It is the delight in your brown eyes, dimmed to anger now and then by hurtful words—Spic, illegal wetback, lazy Mexican—a pittance of words thrown your way by those who have wasted a lifetime holding their hat in hand, meekly submitting to their weaker impulses.

True, you were never one to work until the last disk in the back turns chalky and you're unable to stand. What you have is the dream for a better life, arriving in Albuquerque that night, lights brimming the sky below as you topped the crest of Nine Mile Hill.

Remember, my son, when one is born new again, the face of the newborn shows no emotion as it peers over the volcano rim, the eruption of its own fate already under way. This fresh beginning feels like death—

you are thrust naked and disarmed into the unseen, abandoned in an open clearing where you have to find your way back to life, reshape yourself in the world, uneasy because what you are seeing frightens you.

A mile-long and mile-wide love you are, shouldering pure-life boy in size and strength, to you I gave the sacred arrowhead. Two hours after your birth I pushed it in beneath the skin over your heart to protect you from harm.

As a teenager you loved to strut about the camp like a rooster with feathers spread, looking for anything to distract you, cavalier about your natural born strength——"Two guys at once?" You'd crow to a crew of newly arrived Mexicans. "You'll never get a better bet, I could be jailed for giving odds like this."

But trouble gathers over your head like a tornado, leveling what stands in the way of its blind passion, and though you wore down the mountain of sorrow of my departure to an inch-size pebble in your palm, other mountains await.

11

April 2002

Vito enjoyed working at the junkyard, especially because it was next to the Rio Grande and something about being by the river made him feel safe and close to his family back at the migrant camp.

On this warm day in April, he ran his hand over an Impala's metal-flake steering wheel and its tuck and roll seats. "Bad," he murmured, "blood even on the baby chair." He felt sick.

He pulled himself out and looked over the acres of mutilated vehicles, shaking his head. He unscrewed a mirror, pulled off the exterior door molding, and piled them on a flatbed truck beside the car. He sprayed WD-40 on rusty bolts, went through the toolbox to find the right ratchet for the screws.

"What're your plans tonight," Ignacio asked, crawling out from under another car.

"I know you're taking Lucia out and you're trying to set me up with her cousin. Puffy eyelids, big old snout that hooks over her upper lip, beady eyes."

"Lucia's mine."

"Women just can't resist me. Man's got to do something with his mind while picking bugs out of his crotch from fucking bush hogs," Vito said.

Ignacio bit his lip trying to understand what Vito was implying. "Whatever. Sure you don't want to double date?"

"Naw, I'll finish this, then chill by the river, check my lines for catfish." Vito pried open the trunk with a tire iron. "Nice," he said, reaching for a pair of black and red boxing gloves with gold braid lace and the initials JC in green on each wrist in the center of a black eagle. "There a pawnshop near here?" he asked, but Ignacio was gone, probably over to the salvage-yard office.

Vito took out the spare tire and jack and discovered a black gym bag. Something slithered backward and was gone—then he saw the rattlesnake, coiled in the trunk. He grabbed the bag and jumped back, slammed the trunk shut. He unzipped the bag, found boxing trunks, speed-bag mitts, a sweatband, a water bottle, and several *Ring* magazines. He went over to the riverbank, lay under a cottonwood tree, and leafed through the magazines.

After a while he put the magazines aside and put his hands under his head and looked up at the sky wondering how his family was doing at the camp. He remembered with fondness the day Carmen appeared.

He and Jose, a Vietnam vet and heavy equipment operator at the camp, had been working steadily through the afternoon until a car pulled up and a woman got out. She wore big black-framed designer sunglasses and her hair parted in ponytails.

Vito idled the scraper and climbed down. He took off his bandanna and she started laughing.

She took off her sunglasses.

"You look," she covered her mouth with her hand, "like an alien with those dirt rings around your eyes and nose." He could just barely see the outline of her breasts under her denim short-sleeved shirt. She had a tawny complexion like a seasoned copper kettle burnished by flame for decades and her large brown eyes looked directly at him.

"Can you tell me where the migrant camp is," she asked.

"Why?"

"I'm doing an internship there."

"Go straight and you'll see the camp and the sheds. Ask for my dad, Casimiro. Tell him I sent you."

For the next two weeks Vito was in heaven. He did everything he could to woo her. He found her a shack to live in by the river. He brought over boxes of fresh fruit and vegetables and gathered up cooking pots and kitchen utensils for her. He organized the local camp women to host a moving-in party. He walked with her, confessed he loved her, that something about her had completely swept him off his feet, and he vowed he would marry her someday.

She tried to calm this headstrong seventeen-year-old kid but it didn't work. Whenever she talked to him, the dreamy, distracted look in his eyes bothered her concentration. He told her stories about camp people and made her laugh, they picnicked on the ditch bank, they walked along the river and watched the geese come and go.

He was filled with joy, certain she was sent by God and that she also felt an intoxicating surge of enlivening energy soar through her. They were two souls meant for each other.

Every morning after a brief encounter at breakfast, he'd climb on the scraper and gorge the dirt, speeding back and forth as if he were racing someone, going faster and faster until he wasn't even slowing down to pick up the dirt—he was just running at it full speed, scooping, closing the bucket, racing across the road, turning sharply around the corner, and dumping the load at full throttle.

This morning, on the third pass, rumbling at full speed, he turned sharply, rounding the corner onto an expanse of barren dirt shaved smooth and clean of prairie vegetation that Mr. Miller was developing into his private golf course. Overtaken by the state of childlike elation, he didn't realize the scraper had hooked the fencing. He kept driving, dragging the fence and ripping out poles until he was dragging a whole length of it behind him.

Jose came running in his direction, pointing to the rear, and Vito turned to see a gnarled mess of fencing. "Holy shit," he gasped, then turned off the ignition and jumped down. The fencing was caught under the universal joints and rear axel. "I gotta get wire cutters, I'll be back."

A half hour later, he approached the site on foot, wondering what Carmen's car was doing parked in the middle of the dirt road.

In front of her car was Miller's '67 Mustang, and he saw Herman, Miller's boy, with a friend, their car blocking hers. When he got within earshot, he heard Herman saying that Mexican girls had nice big asses, which Vito thought was true and liked, but it was the derisive tone and their refusal to let her pass that got him pissed.

He walked up and ordered them to let her go. He was hot, thirsty, and ill tempered.

"We're just having a little fun," Herman sneered. "Wanna see her clap and dance like them Spanish senoritas and shake them belugas."

"How about I dance my foot up in your ass?" Vito stared at them.

Herman's fun voice changed to a cold scowl. "You better remember who I am and who you work for, Mexican, before you start throwing threats around."

"You don't threaten us," Herman's red-haired friend snarled.

When Vito came out of his rage, the two kids were on the ground, swollen eyed, purple cheeked, and with lips bleeding. He was standing with his fists still clenched, breathing hard.

Around seven that night headlights bobbed down the dirt road alongside the chili fields toward the camp and Casimiro's place. Miller pulled up, honked, and when Casimiro came out he motioned him over to the driver's-side window. After Miller left, Vito asked what had happened, and his father told him, "He wants you out."

They looked into each other's eyes and sensed the life-changing moment. Casimiro knew Vito had done what he was supposed to do as a man and Vito knew he had put his family's future on the line. And he and Casimiro stood there taking in a long moment of life's sorrow.

12

March 2002

Casimiro sent Vito to work in the junkyard in Albuquerque for his good friend Rafael. Vito had been working about three weeks, dismantling wrecked cars for parts that were still usable, when Rafael sent Vito and Ignacio on a call to pick up old scaffolding.

When they arrived, workers were stuccoing, buffing wood floors, painting, and running wire for electricity. The yard was filled with junk and one of the guys directed them to the pile of scaffolds.

Once they were done loading them, Vito went inside to the bathroom and Ignacio struck up a conversation with a pretty blonde girl. When Vito came back outside he found a flyer and a weekly rag pinned under the wiper blades of the truck. While he sat in the cab waiting for Ignacio, he leafed through the tabloid. The headlines on every page were about atrocities along the border: drug wars, ten people killed a day, over four hundred women raped and murdered, INS arresting thousands of Mexicans without documents, deporting thousands more, new prisons being built along the border to imprison Mexicans. The articles were accompanied by photos of children working in the fields, dismembered women, and slain law enforcement officials.

He scanned the flyer. It was a call for people to attend an upcoming rally in support of a muralist—a local hero who, after living in America for more than thirty years, had been deported. The INS split the family up and the children were left in America while the father and mother were arrested and shipped off to Mexico.

The flyer went on:

Have you ever wondered why the media depicts us as drug dealers, why they think we suck blood from the economy? We've been low-wage slaves for the rich too long!!

Break the habit of believing them when they tell us they're doing what they do to us for our own good! It's time to speak up, show our force, our power! Show your support tomorrow at the protest march at 10:00 a.m. at Tiquex Park. We've had enough of people stepping on us!! We're citizens and we deserve all the rights due to citizens.

Ignacio jumped in and exclaimed, "I got her number, let's go." He looked at Vito. "What the hell's that?"

"This paper, they're right."

Ignacio took it and read. "Shit, they got these rallies every weekend. Fuck that shit. Blow it off, man, it's bullshit, we got better things to do this weekend." He shook the girl's phone number in his fist and repeated, "Yeah, brother, much better things."

Vito folded the flyer up, slid it in his back pocket, and started driving back to the salvage yard.

"Don't you know that selling hope is the best hustle there is."

"What you talking about, bro?"

"Life is suffering, all of life. Whatever, dude, I won't be suffering tomorrow with Yolanda." He held up the scrap of paper with her number scribbled on it.

They drove in silence, crossing Rio Bravo and heading north on Second Street, the railroad on their right, the river on their left. Vito was checking out the new Roadrunner commuter train that had just pulled into the station. It ran between Belen and Santa Fe. Suddenly, Ignacio yelled, "Fuck, watch out!"

Vito slammed the brakes to avoid crashing into the back end of a black Escalade that had slowed almost to a stop at the railroad tracks. Scaffolding sailed over the top of the truck and smashed into the Escalade's rear window.

The Escalade's door opened and a man dressed in a silk suit stepped out.

Ignacio moaned, "Oh shit."

It was Puro, a Mafia gangster who controlled all the strip clubs in Albuquerque.

Ignacio ran his index finger across his lips, warning Vito not to say anything smart.

Puro yelled, "Son of a bitch!" He slammed his door and approached the truck, then pounded the hood with a closed fist.

He glared at Vito. "What's the fucking rush?" Puro raised both arms up as if he were being robbed and did a full spin, "Shit, shit, shit. Nothing but bad news today. Bad, bad, bad." He motioned Vito to step out but Vito sat motionless.

He lunged and grabbed Vito's shirt through the open window. He started to drag him out then he recognized Ignacio. He stepped back, brushed himself off, and backed away from the truck. "You work for Rafael?"

"I'll pay for it, calm down." Vito got out of the truck, meeting Puro's stare.

"How we going to do this, then?" Every molecule in Puro's brain calculated the value of Vito's existence. He exhaled. "People move ahead in life with luck, work, or risk. Which is it with you?"

"Risk." Vito could feel that Puro was impressed by his lack of fear and his calm demeanor.

Puro gazed up at heaven as if asking the angels to intercede, then looked at Vito and repeated, "How we gonna do this, then?"

"You tell me," Vito countered, motioning toward the smashed window.

Puro looked him over for a few minutes, then asked, "You box?"

The question caught Vito off guard. "You want to settle the score now?"

"No, I mean in the ring." He laughed easily, slapping Vito's arm roughly.

"Sure." Vito said.

A spark of connection was lit between the two.

"Meet me tonight at the old redbrick rail-yard bar at eight. A four rounder. You win, you've paid the tab; you lose, you pay me double." He gestured toward the window of his Escalade.

"I win, we're square."

Puro winked. "That's it, kid."

Vito and Ignacio reloaded the rebar. The afternoon heat was intense as Vito coaxed the gears through first, second, and third and drove on to the junkyard.

He was going to night school to get his GED and even though he'd committed to going to class and seeing it through, missing one night wouldn't hurt. He'd make up for it.

He thought about the boxing gloves he had found a few days earlier and how he had never made much out of coincidences like this. In the past, to his mind, field-workers attributing God's intervention to winning a couple of hundred dollars at bingo was naive and ridiculous. Yet now he wasn't so sure. His life had always been filled with jumbled situations, touched by chaos, but now it did seem like God or some divine power had an intention for him, a beneficent intention. The gloves were a sign from God, showing him what he was supposed be doing with his life. Somebody was throwing good juju at him and he was going to take it as long as it lasted.

13

It was March 19, Saturday evening, and that night Vito swung
the gym bag over his shoulder like a gunslinger and strutted into
the bar. His life would change forever this evening.

It was a generic Mexican bar that sold cheap wine and beer
and there were a few whiskey bottles on glass shelves that were
otherwise almost all empty. A ring was set up in back. The songs
on the jukebox were oldies but goodies from the fifties and sixties. The place was buzzing with workers still in their work
clothes, sunburned and looking like they didn't want to hear any
bullshit. Women laughed loudly.

They sat at the bar. Ignacio nudged his side. *"Me gusta esa
jaina,"* he said, raising his eyebrows toward the bartender's ass
wrapped in tight black jeans. Chili-pepper lights dangled, cast-
ing red shadows on the ceiling, giving the place a neglected feel,
a drunk's Christmas remorse.

A long mirror ran the length of the wall, above shelves
stacked four deep with dozens of different tequilas. Sleazy flea-
market pictures of naked women in sombreros and gun belts hung
at either end.

They ordered drinks.

The boxing ring in the back was red, the ropes blue. In
black leather booths suited men and flashy women sipped

expensive tequila. Weathered cowboys, cocaine lawyers, glaze-eyed potheads, homeboy policemen, drug dealers, and citizens usually in bed after the evening news, all crowded the tables and filled the steel folding chairs around the ring.

He spotted his opponent. A muscular black guy flaunting an American flag bracelet and gold earrings, with long braids of his cornrows interwoven with silver wire; brawny and chiseled and as wide as he was tall. He sported a black panther tattoo on his forearm and his two front gold teeth flashed diamonds to match the shimmering, tall, blonde woman at his side. Fans gathered around paying tribute.

Vito was pumped up and excited by this forbidden world. With the exception of accompanying his mother to the bar where she used to sing, this was the first bar he'd ever been in. His father hated places like this. Before coming to Albuquerque, Vito hardly ever went beyond the camp's boundaries. And his father constantly warned against hanging out with hoodlums and hustlers. Now he took it all in.

"Gotta get a little excitement here," Vito yelled, spouting off contemptuous provocations in the black man's direction. "You better believe in spirits, that's the only help you're getting tonight."

The black boxer didn't get worked up by the taunt. He stepped closer to Vito to intimidate him but his Filipino cornerman blocked his way, holding him at arm's length.

The confrontation revved the crowd. They whistled for the boxers to get it on and it spurred Vito. "I'm the reason it rains, puddy. You should have put a bowl of water under your bed last night to ward off evil 'cause you're going on your knees tonight sucka, two knees, not one."

Vito caught sight of Puro out of the corner of his eye, sitting in a booth, and Puro's hand slid across his throat, gesturing to Vito to cut the crap.

In the men's bathroom he changed into his gear. Ignacio laced up Vito's gloves—the ones he had found in the car trunk.

He said to Ignacio, "I wonder what the initials on the gloves stand for."

He imagined the kid's last moment—a sunburst eruption of burning steel, ripped bolts, and shattered glass, airborne, grinding noise spinning to a halt. Blood, panic, terror, pain, and charred regret, then the inexorable lightness of floating above this life, into the land of spirits. He kissed the gloves to show respect.

When Vito came out, the black fighter was waiting, looking all of a million dollars and change, decked out in a silver cape with matching gloves and shoes, face shining with grease, a gold medallion that read STUD hanging from his neck.

Vito climbed into the ring and said, "No U-turns! This is going to be a Sunday sightseeing drive for me. I'm putting it on cruise control." He smacked his gloves and lunged at Stud, who didn't move, and as the ref warned Vito no more antics or he'd risk forfeiting, Stud mad-dogged Vito, eyes brewing a savage poison. The ref shoved Vito to his corner and he turned around to face the spectators, lowering his head to pray, when all of a sudden an older woman two rows back from ringside shrieked.

"He's got Johnny's gloves! Take them off!" and she collapsed into tears of agony.

"Must be the kid's mother," Ignacio said.

Just as the ref ordered Vito to the middle of the ring for instructions, the woman started clawing to free herself from her husband, yelling, "Take them off!"

Vito climbed over the ropes, made his way to them, and knelt next to the couple. "I found them in a car at the junkyard I work at. Maybe it's his way, you know, of doing something through me, like he wants to fight again. Please, let me use them. I'm sorry, just let me use them, just tonight."

The father patted his wife's shoulder, consoling her. "It's okay, honey, calm down. Let him fight for our boy, just tonight."

The woman moaned into her cupped hands, then wiped her tears, gulping her breath. "Okay, okay."

The ref yelled, "Is the visit over?" A pause. "Or are you forfeiting?"

Vito leaned in, "I'll bring him honor . . . *me la rayo.*" I promise. The mother pressed her fingers to her lips and rubbed the initials.

The bell rang.

Vito danced, bobbing in and out buoyantly, showing off the ease he had avoiding the slugger's punches, smiling at the spectators, until the first blow connected and Stud decked him. Bleary eyed, seeing fuzzy twos, head floating light with bath bubbles, not sure what had happened, he rose wobbly kneed.

Stud sighted him in the crosshairs of his rage and beat him down, growling, "I want to marry you, let the world know you're my bride. Say you're this nigger's chili-pie bride, Mezz-kin. Mine." All Vito could do was cover up, back against the ropes, protect his face, and flinch with each blow to his body.

"Wear you on my arm like a shirt, bitch. Sing to me, bitch, sing to me," and Stud kept pounding him in the ribs and lower back without mercy.

As he was being beat he heard a back door open and felt a fresh night breeze sweep through the bar. Someone outside cried in Spanish to grab a chicken and cook it. A radio blared "Flor de las Flores." People ordered drinks, moved table to table, and huddled in areas between tables. Their chatter, rising in English and Spanish, pitched against his ears with the festive rhythms of a holiday.

Lungs smoldering and puffing short breaths, eyes burning like dry pine needles in fire, he found himself looking down at the people as if the ring he was standing in was the mountain peak center of the world.

Stud's brutal punches drove him over waterfalls, cooling the chili powder in his wounds, over cliffs, bouncing him until he was borne aloft, floating through air with a deafening roar in his heart that blocked everything else out. He turned end over end and splashed down into this moment, soaked in his perspiration, yelping in pain, swinging his right fist in the air to ward off the blows, until he felt himself lift off the bottom, an inflatable raft carrying him up from the dark drowning depths.

He glimpsed Stud's menacing face grinning through the water, his features wavering and watery. He couldn't breathe. He struggled to swim but Stud pushed him down, down, until he felt he was losing consciousness and as he floated lifelessly down he vaguely remembered studying the gloves, the green leather, the beautiful initials embossed in yellow stitching.

He was outside himself, watching himself go down to the murky bottom when the gloves pulled his arms out and up like a spring that shot him up streaming past the water. He coughed, he flung his head back and forth, and in a raging trance he pounded Stud's face down to the ground.

He'd never taken a beating like that and when the bell rang, Ignacio had to enter the ring and escort Vito to the corner. He was dazed, his face cut, bruised purple, and red with broken blood vessels.

Hecklers cajoled him as another wannabe boxer.

"I'm throwing it in," Ignacio said.

Vito cringed through the slits of his swollen eyelids—they were distended and discolored black and blue—shaking his head no. He looked at the crowd jeering and howling, enjoying his beat-down. His eyes rested on the parents. The father motioned his right arm toward his jaw, swinging it up several times. The mother swung her fist sideways, telling him to use a crossover. He saw Puro shaking his head in disgust and when their eyes met Puro ran his finger under his neck, ordering him to stop the fight.

All of them expected him to lose—except for the kid's parents—and it pissed Vito off.

"Bring in the cows 'cause winter is coming on." He slapped his gloves. "Come on lil' doggie."

Ignacio wiped blood from his face, lubricated his cuts with Vaseline, and poured water over his head. "You sure, *carnal*, there's always another day."

"Call me Mr. Blacksmith," Vito grinned. "Time to melt down some scrap iron." Ignacio, not knowing what he was talking about, shoved the mouthpiece in and grunted with confidence, "Go get 'em blacksmith." Vito winced, the pain in his jaw and ribs stinging.

Stud's gold teeth gleamed as he stood and scoffed, "After this I'm going to have ten gold teeth."

Just as the bell sounded for the second round, the phone rang at Rafael's house. He was tired and ready to get into bed, watch the 10:00 p.m. news and hit the sack. He answered the phone. It was Lorenzo, informing him Casimiro had had a stroke.

Rafael put on his boots, cap, and coat and drove to meet Vito at his GED class and maybe take him out to the pancake house and talk. On his way there, he passed the bar and pulled in, curious why the truck was parked in front and not at school. He entered the bar, greeted a few old friends, and froze when he saw Vito in the ring.

He'd promised Casimiro he'd take care of Vito, guide him as a mentor would, teach him responsibility, and get him to graduate night school. And as soon as he saw Puro, it all came together. He was incensed.

He'd known Puro for years and knew he was one to exploit an opportunity to make money, no matter the cost. Somehow Puro had trapped Vito in his web. Getting a young, impressionable kid on his side, especially one as big and strong as Vito, might put some money in his pocket, despite the damage it would do to Vito. But Rafael had given his word to Casimiro and that bothered him more than anything; his integrity had now been drawn into doubt and dragged through the dirt by this . . . son of a bitch.

Puro was leaning against the wall when Rafael shoved him, at the same time grabbing his hand and stopping Puro from going for his waistline gun. Rafael seethed, "Keep your hands off this kid."

Their eyes probed each other's like the children they used to be when they climbed up in the trees at night and stole apples, each wondering if the noise they heard was Mr. Javier coming out of his house. It was fear in their eyes under the moon back then, and fear now in both their eyes that something was happening they couldn't stop. It was like that with passions that open up gates of fury or love, changing lives forever.

The fans hardly noticed them, so enraptured were they by the turn of events in the ring. After the first round, many had paid their tab intent on leaving, but now the chairs were occupied. Suddenly the crowd was on its feet, high-fiving a clean punch to the jaw, which was countered with a crushing blow to the ribcage. They were whipped into a frenzy at Vito's comeback.

"Look at him compadre," Puro begged. "Look, first time he's boxed. It's incredible."

And Rafael turned and saw Vito smack Stud at will, wearing him down to a thin wafer of submission. He was intimidating now, stepping almost daintily and looking around with fierce black eyes, burning a dark fire hotter than blue and white flame, his eyes demanding tribute of one who knows that nothing can resist fire. He hopped and skipped around the ring, a young lion over a wounded doe, or a sparrow with its first straw for its nest.

Rafael gasped, struck with such force by the sight of Vito pummeling his opponent with powerful uppercuts that sent Stud sprawling out of the ring. He turned and left just as the ref stopped the fight.

The dark, the cigarette smoke, the lamps illuminating the ring, the stench of sweat and reek of perfume and cologne, the shoulder-to-shoulder crowd saw it and for a moment an underwater silence overtook everyone and no one breathed. Each brain clocked the last punch that was, alone, worth the money they paid to get in.

Vito had been smacked down and was losing badly, humiliated by a clubhouse draft horse, as vulnerable and defenseless as a bird on the ground with a bad wing. He tasted the air exhaled from the smoking and drinking crowd, knew he could fly, and rose to a call in his blood greater than him, greater than the sum of all those in the bar cheering every punch his adversary smashed into his jaw, ribs, arms, chin, head, and stomach.

As he stood there staring at Stud on the floor, he spit to the side, sweat and blood shimmering down his face and chest, heart shouting for more violence. He slapped the dead boy's gloves together, yelling for Stud to get up. He wanted to hit and get hit, duck and catch shots, block, counterpunch, get stunned by an uppercut and sting back with a left hook, sweat flying and spraying into the crowd, blood spattering the floor. He relished it, he exulted in it, it was his element, where fire was born, fire was used, and air and earth and water streamed through his gloves to make him an element of earth that could not be dominated, bent, broken, or tamed.

Sixty or seventy fans heaved in waves into the ring, squashing him with offered drinks and cigars, reaching over each other to touch any part of him. He couldn't move, dizzy with head-splitting pain. He was coming back, returning to the place and time but still withdrawn; fans seemed a blurred nest of buzzing flies joyfully feasting on horse shit.

I told you, he thought, talking to the dead boxer. The win is mine, but it's yours, too. Those motherfuckers, he thought, and kissed the gloves, and to the spirit boxer he thought, I told you I'd honor you. You took me to the water's edge and I stepped up on the shore. You gave your gloves the music of war, all I had to do was move them and horses charged forth from each one. I felt it when you pulled me up. *Gracias.*

Part Two

14

Ah, my man Casimiro, all those people you loved as a boy and had faith in that they could deliver you from poverty. They told you keep your sights high and described the wonders of America and how life could be if you worked hard and trusted in the American dream. It will never let you down, they said, and you rose early and went to bed knowing the words were true as the ten commandments and that you had a life waiting for you beyond the border.

All you had to do was cross miles of desert, hide from Blackwater assassins and Blackwater mercenaries and keep moving north along sandy ravines, burying yourself in dirt to sleep, because you believed in what they said.

But over the years you became a man without hope, without a single wish that came true, and that hurts more than anything in the world and it can never be erased because that was all you ever talked about, about the promised land under stars. Believing what they told you opened your heart and you would have done anything for them and you did, you gave it all up to follow them, and the lies broke you. It was not as they said, you were no longer who you were. Despair and darkness poured out of your eyes and there was nothing you could do about it. You were completely powerless to even whisper a complaint and you carried this dark need to avenge the betrayal, to devour people and destroy, to make people pay for what they had said, make them suffer, and that was what you hated most, because you are a good man, and became not much of anything.

The soil of your soul, the soil of your breath, the soil of your words extinguishes the fire of your life, blows and rearranges your days to become another's story and with every retelling a new detail is imagined, another diamond added to map your transformation.

One son works in the fields and another son's face blows in the breeze—Vito's black hair waving over his eyes and mouth, his lips grim as he watches you wave good-bye.

I know, my love, I know. As mist drifts over the fields around the camp and you inhale its musk, staring into the glint leaf of a new morning, remember my love, do not escape hardship through the trapdoor of a bitter dream deferred.

15

March 2003

After doing a few chores on a Saturday afternoon, it was too hot to work in the warehouse and Casimiro decided to wait until it cooled a bit. He relaxed in the doorway of the Pullman and picked at the calluses on his palms, looking over the fields toward the river, wondering how Rafael and Vito were doing and feeling that maybe it would all turn out for the better. If anybody could tame a young colt, it was Rafael. They had worked side by side in the rows and there was no one better at working than Rafael. He was the only one he could trust with his son's welfare and it was fitting because he had waited outside the door the whole time during Nopal's labor until Vito was born and because of that Casimiro considered him Vito's godfather.

Thinking with pleasure about Lorenzo's first birthday, Casimiro then remembered how, eleven months after they had met, on a Thursday morning, Nopal's water broke. While the women escorted her to Elena, the midwife, Casimiro carefully cut the plants the midwife had anointed and placed them to dry on the Pullman windowsill. Then, he crushed and burned them, waving the smoke around the railcar as he prayed to the spirits to care for his wife and infant.

A year passed and they celebrated their baby's first birthday by walking to the river and eating watermelon. Casimiro held his son's tiny hand in his as the child toddled across the fields. Lorenzo lurched excitedly over the rows, his wobbly head weighing more than his body, no taller than a plant. He yelped at everything he saw, heard, or sniffed, pausing now and then to read his parent's eyes for signs of danger.

Casimiro had felt sad that his son was going to be a slave to the fields, too, but before he could tell his wife he was sorry, that he'd work harder to make sure he would go to school in the city, thinking how to say to Nopal that he had more than paid for his son's freedom with his sweat, she surprised him with the news that she was pregnant again.

After a while, Casimiro got up and he walked out to the field to check the irrigation water. He didn't want it going over the rows into the road. He heard the dirt murmuring Nopal's name up at him.

He suddenly felt flushed with heat, nauseated. His arm ached, his vision blurred. His head hurt. He walked slowly over to the water truck, pulled the freezing ladle from the ice-filled cooler, and drank heartily as some of the water dribbled down his mouth, onto his shirt. After wiping his mouth with his forearm, he lit a cigarette, and with the greatest pleasure exhaled the smoke out on the air. Still, his face felt feverish and he poured water over his head, drenched his handkerchief and draped it over his head, and he fell down and found that he couldn't get up.

★ ★ ★

The puppet strings holding him up were cut and with all his strength he tried to move, closing his fingers into a fist and using it as a support to rise but it didn't work. He gave a heaving moan of frustration and fear. Scratching at mud, he licked his lips and tasted the dirt he had been working his whole life. Dizzy and disoriented, he rolled over, stared at the sky, told himself to breathe deep and relax. When the spell was finally over, he rose and looked around to make sure no one had seen what had just happened.

He was scared but there was a solution for fear and he headed to the shed, cranked up the tractor, and drove to the fields even though it was Sunday. Work was always the answer.

Then, on a Thursday afternoon, twelve days after his fall, the perfectly blue sky filled with migrating cranes and the chili plants vibrant and stalwart, feeling robust and carrying a sack of green chili to the truck, Casimiro collapsed. Lorenzo rushed him to the rural clinic nine miles away but the doctor only showed up on Mondays. By the time they arrived in Las Cruces, twenty-two miles away, the right half of Casimiro's body was paralyzed, his mouth drooped, his leg and arm dangled inert, and his speech had become a series of mumbles and slurs. His face was slack as if a weighted hook was pulling down on it, dangling from the right side, giving him a grotesque grin and twisting the flesh of his right eye and half his mouth into a snarl.

★　★　★

Casimiro was confined to the wheelchair Lorenzo bought at a second-hand store and during the next few weeks the son parked his father next to the water bucket on the truck, where the workers who huddled around could greet him and share the latest gossip.

Sitting in his wheelchair, he studied insects, birds, and flowers, amazed they had no sense of greed or envy or hate. In the space of an hour he saw dragonflies, wasps, crickets, praying mantises, stink bugs, fireflies, ladybugs, mosquitoes, and grasshoppers. They reminded him of when Vito was a child playing near the creek, capturing insects in a mason jar to use as fish bait.

With his left hand he reached into the cooler next to his wheelchair and pulled out a bottle of ice water. He placed it in the cup holder and backed the left wheel to reverse his chair out of the sun. The cold water chilled his brain, numbed his throat.

Around ten in the morning the workers headed to the truck for a water break, tossing their bags and hoes down, lining up to dip the ladle into the blue-black water in the pine barrel and gulp great scoops of water until it drenched their chins and chests.

Behind Casimiro, someone opened the passenger door on the other side of the truck and punched the glove box to get it open.

"*Papa, dónde están los Band-aids?*" Lorenzo asked.

"*Abajo el sillon,* on the driver's side," the words were shredded, almost unintelligible, but Lorenzo could make them out.

Lorenzo pulled the white first-aid box out from under the seat and rummaged through it, grabbing as many Band-aids as he could find. "New ones signed on this morning, soft hands. I tell them we don't work by the clock, we work by the light. Blisters." He smiled, "*Bueno,* papa, gotta go."

"I miss him," Casimiro grumbled.

Lorenzo saw his father's left hand shaking uncontrollably. He felt he had to do something soon, but it took money, lots of it.

Casimiro watched him. Lorenzo's shoulders slumped, his back was a little stooped. The fields were wearing down his boy.

For an instant Casimiro felt that today might be the day when everything suffered turns out for the better, when God comes down on the earth and stands beside him, touches his arthritic hands and appreciates the work he's done; today an angel descends and rewards him for his fairness to workers and kindness to children, today blessings will spill over his hands and legs, flooding over the field irrigation gates, brimming the rows, and no longer will despair attend him like an angry choke hold at his throat. But most of all, today is the day when Vito settles down and gets rid of his wildness, and the curse of the dream is lifted from Lorenzo.

16

June 2003

After Casimiro's stroke, Lorenzo took over the operations of the camp. He was well-known and respected. He had foremen and forewomen under him to whom he delegated day-to-day duties but he assumed ultimate responsibility for everything including disking fields at appropriate times for dormancy or seeding, supervising the field crew, overseeing the women in the warehouse who were boxing and shipping out the chili, paying the workers each Friday, and keeping up the maintenance of farm machinery.

Most importantly, informing all his duties was the unspoken authority he carried in his demeanor, his genuine care and protection of the people who resided in the camp. He looked after them. They sought out his knowledge on legal matters and his advice on their children's education, health care, and administrative issues dealing with their legal or illegal status in America. They asked him for suggestions about their permits and for news on the immigration service. Whether it was an ailing child, a residency question, or an incident in town where one claimed to be cheated or was arrested, he dealt with them with compassion and concern.

★　★　★

Now, as a crop duster buzzed over the fields, Lorenzo and Carmen pulled up to the warehouse, jumped out of the truck, and started hefting fifty-pound sacks of chili from the truck bed to a wagon stationed at the loading dock. A worker swung her legs off the office desk where she was sitting and ran up the ramp to help weigh the gunnysacks, writing the weights down on a clipboard, stacking the bags in another pile, and pulling the heaping wagon into the warehouse where conveyor belts hummed, hydraulic motors groaned, and dozens of workers silently focused on packing, cleaning, and inspecting chili.

"We make a pretty good team," Carmen said proudly as they walked into the warehouse. Rays of sun shot through broken boards and loose roof tin into the warehouse, golden light slanting across the faces of the men, women, and children standing at the conveyor belt. The fragrance of green chili floated through the huge front doors where tractors and produce trucks arrived to unload supplies or pack up produce boxes for shipment.

From time to time animals would appear in the warehouse and the children would scamper after them to shoo them out but the chickens, ducks, dogs, mice, and rabbits would scurry into the pile of cardboard boxes or under straw and into shadowy corners.

For the first two weeks that Carmen worked the belt, her hands burned, her lungs were irritated, she coughed all the time, and her eyes swelled up and reddened from the stinging dust.

No matter how many times she washed her hands, blew her nose, or drank water, her eyes were on fire, her throat was always raw and her sinuses aflame, and she emptied endless Kleenex boxes sneezing and sniffling.

"Come on, we have to feed my horse," Lorenzo said.

They walked across the compound to the corral by the Pullman and tossed sheaves of hay over the fence to Lorenzo's horse. Then they leaned on the corral and watched the horse tear into the hay.

"I wrote my mom about staying on and she doesn't like it. She says six weeks is long enough. My dad's cool with it, though."

"Why would it worry her?"

"She planned on me going back to school. You know, hooking up with a doctor, not hanging out with field hands. Everything's an investment to her. She paid for private schools, ballet, music lessons, study abroad."

"She thinks you're wasting your life out here?"

"Yep. She'd go nuts if she knew I wash my clothes in a tub and dry them on a clothesline. She'd go even crazier if she knew I was falling for someone."

After a bit of silence, she laughed. "You're blushing."

"I'm not." He paused and then changed the subject. "And if she knew you cook for the old ones who can't, tutor kids in English, write letters to their families in Mexico, chauffeur women to the post office?"

"She'd send the police and claim I'd been brainwashed." She bent and turned on the spigot and drank from it. Water splashed on her hair and face and stuck her T-shirt to her nipples.

He couldn't help but stare as she slid between the corral fencing and went into the corral to brush his horse down.

"Did you know that in the Mayan culture virgins could pick their lovers. The man had no say in it," she said clenching the rope tighter as the horse shied. After a bit, she said, "Let's get a beer sometime, maybe at the place your mother used to sing at?"

"Sure, it's about ten miles south, down by the river."

17

It was the first time in years Lorenzo had visited the place. He and Carmen pulled into the dirt lot in front of the weather-blistered cinder block building. The Russian olive tree next to the plank door gave off a beggar's air, its spindly limbs caked in white chalk from desert winds sanding the cinder bricks. Black birds and prairie doves nested in empty tar buckets on the flat roof and black mops and rubber boots added to the clutter. It was early evening and already a group of men stood around outside drinking ice cold beer. Dogs panted under trucks, pigeons lined up on utility lines, and frogs croaked from the ditch behind the bar.

When a man opened the door to join the others inside, Lorenzo could hear Lola Beltrán's "Tu Solo Tu" wailing from the jukebox. La Suerte, as the place was now called, had the menu written on a plywood board outside, next to the door: *carne asada, menudo, posole, al pastor, pollo en mole, carnitas, chili verde, birria, lengua, barbacoa y lonches Mexicanos.*

The front part of the bar was a store. Inside, ceiling fans turned slowly, the blades encrusted with dead mosquitoes and yellow jackets. A young Arab who had come across the border through Juárez a few years earlier stood behind the display case next to the register, talking in Urdu as he rang up calling cards for Mexican customers. Against the wall behind him shelves laddered up to the ceiling, sagging with dusty Mexican canned goods, knives, cowboy hats, leather belts, magic cures in green bottles, hex herbs, and bone-chip relics from mestizo saints in tiny plastic bags.

Down two aisles, at the back end of the store, workers waited for their food orders as two aproned cooks turned over steaks, sizzled chili, onion, and garlic on the stove, and set platters piled with huge burritos and tacos wrapped in tinfoil on the stainless steel counter as they called out numbers.

Carmen and Lorenzo walked past the aisles and ducked through a curtained doorway that opened to a spacious dance hall whose ceiling and walls depicted faded murals of scenes from the Mexican revolution. Light streaks from bullet holes in the ceiling struck the dark interior, illuminating the tiny airborne specks of field dirt shaken free from clothes and boots. The smell of sweat was engrained in the walls and ceiling.

"There," he pointed, "between the candles."

Carmen went over to the bar and stood under a paddle fan slowly swirling above a blue lamp on a shelf illuminating a photo of his mother.

A wide-hipped waitress approached them. "*Qué quieres?*" She eyed Carmen with the slightly hostile disregard they reserved for outsiders.

They drank their beers in silence until their tacos came and then they ate listening to Amalia Mendoza stir their blood with the passionate yearning of "Le Pido Al Tiempo Que Vuelva."

Carmen loved it. Lorenzo became very sexy—the hot greasy food, the music, the place, the people; it was all so different from her other life.

Scattered around the dance hall, men in T-shirts and jeans sipped beer, eating Wednesday's *barbacoa y chili verde* special, their eyes trolling side to side for someone they knew. She watched them tear off pieces of tortilla and wedge the pieces between thumb and fingers to scoop up the green chili and barbecue meat. They made it look so delicious. Besides pepper and salt, each table held a full bowl of hot salsa and chips.

She saw Lorenzo's jaw muscles clench and unclench; he bit his lip and cracked his knuckles. She knew he was back there again.

His mother mounted the stage and the hall quieted; for a fraction of a second everyone held their breath as her first lines launched lyrics groaning with flammable impulse. And after a few songs, hips swiveling sultry hot in her miniskirt, grinding and stamping her heels on the stage, men yearning for her attention lined up drinks for her at the counter, which she gave away to anyone without money.

And even though Carmen was only beginning to know him, she could tell that memories of his mother's life were still very much alive in his heart and hard for him to relive. His eyelids fluttered, his head turned one way and then the other, he cast his eyes down, then around, and back to his fingers picking at his cuticles, doing what he could to endure the hurt of her death.

"You know," he started, "the temperature hit one hundred eleven yesterday and in Arizona it was worse—they found three dead bodies in the desert, all women. May 25, ought to be a day of mourning, but who gives a shit?"

She motioned the waitress over and ordered two double shots of Chinaco tequila. She wished she could slip under his scalp and she momentarily imagined herself in his brain, swallowed up by his memories.

He continued, "You're a writer, I mean researching your paper on us—maybe you'll write about the panty trees, the trees in the desert with panties in the branches, hundreds of them, each from a woman some bastard Mexican drug smuggler raped. Or about the secret prisons ICE has built in the desert along the border. No one is allowed in—it's Guantánamo Bay or Abu Ghraib on American soil. Thousands of Mexicans arrested and confined there. Nobody fucking cares."

He was trying to control his anger but couldn't. "Three blacks in Texas are dragged behind a pickup and die, and it's headlines around the world; white kids in Utah are kidnapped and it's on every news channel, but Mexicans? Nobody gives a shit."

She knew why he was angry—his mother had been murdered out back behind the bar and all that buried sorrow had fermented into the rage that was now rising up in him.

She said, "Let's do the interview later and just enjoy ourselves now."

He watched a man spit sunflower seeds with expert aim into a Styrofoam cup three feet away. A moth fluttered past a ceiling light. Someone left the back door open and a sparrow flew in, skimming below the ceiling. Kids cheered out back.

The waitress set the tequilas down and he paid.

A group of neatly groomed cowboys walked in: neckerchiefs tied around their collars, new Stetson cowboy hats, tight-fitting jeans, colorful boots—some lime green, some red, some black. They sat down, cleaned their fingernails with pocketknives, shifted toothpicks between their teeth. They were recent arrivals, were wearing their first paychecks.

"So, tell me more about this paper of yours."

"Well, it's not just a paper, it's my dissertation. Basically everything I've done in the last four years. But if you want to really know, it's on communities under duress—that is, how oppression and poverty affect language and culture. What factors contribute to making a community a community."

He ran his tongue inside his cheek, gave a *hmm,* and nodded his head in appreciation. "That explains it," he said, and offered a toast. "To your success," and slugged his shot down. The sting made him grunt. "You think it'll change anything?" This came out with a trace of ridicule.

"It has to. It *will* change things," she said with conviction. Tears started forming in her eyes.

"Come on, baby, we're going to have fun. I'll show you how us Chicanos can dance." He pulled her onto the dance floor, clapped his hands above his head, whirled her around, locked his hands with hers, and rocked her in the rhythm of his bronc-riding hips, shaking to the beat through three songs—Ramon

Ayala's "Cora, Cora," Vicente's "# 1 Interpreter of Life," and
Jose Alfredo Jimenez's "Composer of Love."

Ice cubes rattled, boots and high heels clicked on the wooden
floor, *carnitas* sizzled in frying pans, beer and whiskey saturated
the air, laughter and hysterical yelps arched up as bodies turned
with the loud music, everyone enjoying the fleeting happiness
of the moment.

18

I appear in your dream, Carmen, to tell you,
You are chosen. Only you can tell this story.
Your intellect has been groomed to speak for those who can't.
It is your gift. Carmen, I accompany you.
They are everywhere on the earth.
In Zimbabwe, Iraq, Afghanistan, Mexico,
Their stories never fit facts,
Never fit theories, polls or statistics.
Go deeper,
Feel the forbidding nightmares of their lives shatter their sound-
    proof days so their voices will be heard.
They are everywhere on the earth,
Breathing a third of the air other people breathe,
Eating a third of the food others eat,
Living in squalid camps in one-tenth of the space others use,
Drinking water in cities others defecate in upstream,
Feeling rich when they enjoy a joke with friends and family at
    their sides.

19

When they got back to the camp, a bonfire by the river was going strong. Two dozen people sat on haunches, logs, bricks or stood. The official score-caller, huddled with other ten- and eleven-year-olds, listening to his transistor radio, announced, "*Gol! Gol!* Mexico scores! Two to one."

"Brazil is threatening," another kid piped up, cracking piñon seeds and spitting the hulls out nervously.

Lorenzo and Carmen joined the circle.

"How's it going?" Juanito, a stout man in his midtwenties, greeted them.

"*Muy bien.*"

"And your interviews?" The young woman who spoke looked no older than sixteen and had a honey-peach complexion and raven-glossy curly hair in a pageboy style.

"Write about that worthless piece-of-shit ex-husband of mine. Takes off in the middle of the night with a girl twenty years younger," a fifty-year-old Chicana quipped, her jowls drooping with a sour scowl.

"You can always take off with me; revenge is the sweetest, they say," a grizzled man flirted, his craggy, hoarse tone backed by years of drinking.

"I don't know why you're so interested," a slender, handsome man in his twenties said. "Us Mexicans complain about being poor but ask how many of us spent our checks on beer."

His friend added, "And we think God is going to deliver us from this shit work."

A man in knee-length jeans and dirty sneakers started tuning his guitar. He ran his fingers up and down the frets, strumming one string, then the next, and said without looking up, "I'll play something to tell a small part of our Chicano story." He hummed beneath their talk.

"Where is the song of Mexicans who are so submissive?" the handsome slender man asked. "Chicano life is unbearable because we make it so. No one is to blame for our miserable lives except ourselves." He looked around. "Eh, where's the story in scurrying away like mice to escape *la migra*?"

"Ah, well," an older man said, "that may be the truth. I was one to lie to myself. I had all the fantasies as a young man, that I was special in my talents, but it turns out I was very common."

Heads nodded.

"That was my experience, too," a white-haired woman agreed.

The warble of an infant breast-feeding sounded in the dark.

They gazed into the fire expecting answers to problems. They were hesitant to share with outsiders but in starts and stops the talk opened up and bounced around.

Someone commented on the cut-rate price of cigarettes at the Isleta reservation in El Paso. Another advised about which slots were hot at the Santa Ana casino three hours north on the other side of Albuquerque. A woman gave the inside scoop on Walmart's specials—diapers, rice, beans, flour. A woman wondered aloud when bingo would come to the camp and someone else said to be sure to remember to renew your worker's permit. Words rose and cooled from each person's mouth, then floated down into the fire and melted.

The man with the guitar tapped his fingers against the sound box.

"Leave it," an old man said, scratching his gray head. He stooped over and tossed a stick into the fire. "God'll see to the songs."

The guitar player was about to sing but plucked softly.

The night smelled of cooling asphalt and exhaustion fell on them like autumn leaves off a looming tree.

A woman furried the cinders with a poker and hot ashes scattered into the air.

Carmen looked at the faces, envious of their intimacy, each familiar with the sorrows of the other's life.

"So, why you here?" a woman asked, her features measured so as not to challenge Carmen but invite her to speak. "You were supposed to do interviews and leave—you've been here a little over three months now."

Carmen said, "Yeah, I kind of fell in love with the place." Eyes turned to Lorenzo and women chuckled. "And to help you guys change things."

"Nothing's changing, *mejita,* except for the worse," a woman said.

Carmen felt stupid for saying what she had, the abyss between them and her widened, and she could feel their disdain toward her. "I just want to make a difference," she ended.

"I like those words," a girl said and stepped out from the dark and Carmen saw that she had no arms. Where limbs were supposed to be, small flaps of skin dangled. She was one of the children marked by pesticide poisoning. The reason Carmen hadn't seen any deformed people before tonight was because the parents kept them hidden inside, away from public eyes.

Carmen didn't know how to respond and felt like there was a large rock crushing her heart.

"There are worse curses than slaving in the fields. To be a coward is one."

She swung her eyes to the speaker, thinking he meant her.

"Ah," a thin man offered, "over time hope drains your heart." He shook his head dismally. "What paradise. Every apple you pick condemns you even deeper into hell."

"You regret—," she half asked.

"Regret?" The man looked at her sharply. "Instead of teaching philosophy, I've become an expert in sadness."

The flames danced over their features and Carmen saw how different each person was—some had a wave of golden-wheat love for the land and their families, some had the windy laughter of a cherry tree, others the anger of a hundred firing squads, but one thing common to them all was they wanted to work for a better life and it was one of the most powerful dreams one could have.

20

December 2003

I was there, in the fire, as they talked and this is what I'd spent my life singing about. My songs were tinged with resignation that things will never change. My words savored their stories of suffering, my lyrics were about eyes looking at the horizon for a son that never comes. Hands to cheeks or brows, they thumb each memory as if it were a coin they rub for luck, rubbed so much it evaporated. I sang of rusty coffee-can hearts that memories were saved in: how and when they arrived, what the journey was like, how they settled in.

And before sleeping each night, each digs up the can and unfolds the handkerchief that keeps the memories protected and they run the coins through their fingers again.

I sang of meaningful pain, important pain. Etched in their facial lines of worry, each word was a rubbed forehead, scratched sore, picked pimple, trimmed mustache, a mother's fingers pulling her child's earlobe, wiping his lips.

I remember newcomers to the fields staked and shoveled foundations to erect scrap-wood shacks. I helped hammer and saw boards, told them my piece of land was the stage, located in the center of the universe. They thought it was a joke but after seeing me on weekends they knew.

Sitting in front of the old cracked mirror in my Pullman, I fluffed and brushed my hair, lotioned my face, brushed my eyelashes, puckered on lipstick, penciled a beauty dot on my right cheek, rolled on snake-diamond net stockings with rose-garters, shimmied into a tight blue dress with a pleated hem. Looking in the mirror at my plump butt, I smiled, my calves smooth as I slipped on candy-apple red heels, perfumed my wrists, tuned my guitar, strummed strings for pitch, and, later, looking as primitive as a tigress, I stomped arrogantly across the stage, my high heels clacking like claws on the boards, so loud it made men growl.

Camp women need to be like this sometimes, earthquake boulders down the dirt paths all around them.

I bared my soul, distilled it down from an armored surface of spikes to the inner bark of a cactus, made it my divining rod, quivering at every heart where it signaled life, where it recognized spirits, and there I let myself sing, my voice a power blossoming over them, waterfall petals that touched the hands and ears and hearts and drew blood from remembering their deep passion, remembering the authenticity with which they once lived.

My singing was my freedom, my radical liberation, my plan to subvert the powerful and challenge the rich, both powerless in my presence.

21

February 2004

On a Saturday afternoon in the compound, Carmen and twelve women sat on benches in the shade and husked white corn, washed spinach, cut squash, shelled green beans, roasted chili on a small makeshift brick and wire grill, and sorted pinto beans while some of their kids hurled rocks at crows in the cottonwoods around the camp. The women wrapped tamales in corn leaves, spooned ground beef and beans into tacos, warmed corn tortillas in a hole in the ground over an open fire grill on the *comal,* rolled burritos, and stirred red and green chili simmering in cast iron pots over the open fire. The posole and menudo steamed, and Carmen opened the meeting.

"I wanted all of you here to discuss forming a committee. A formal committee to file grievances on behalf of the workers and present them to Mr. Miller."

The women bowed their heads down as if intent on their work.

"What's wrong?"

Martina swept a pile of corn husks to her side of the table where she was rolling dough, masa, for tamales. Her friend Refugia kneaded the masa and filled it with strips of beef and red and green chili and Martina wrapped corn husks around it. "Carmen, this committee's going to get us in trouble."

"We have families in Mexico who depend on our money every week," Nestora, an older woman said.

The women mumbled assent.

Nestora continued, "The problem will be the men." She lit a cigarette, blew the smoke out, and stared at the sky over the fields, shaking her head slightly at what she was thinking. "Men are always the problem."

"I don't have time for it," Lydia said, "unless the committee can help me with Maria's *quinceañera* this month. She's fifteen."

"And maybe the committee can help with Juanito's baptism," Elaine said.

"We'll have to make a big barbecue, sew the dresses," Lydia added.

Carmen asked, "Why do you serve others and never worry about your own needs? This could make it better for your families."

They gazed at her with endearment, puzzled by her idealism.

"I mean, you allow others to exploit and use you and yet it doesn't seem like you even care."

And then the youngest of the women, Christina, who seldom spoke, said, "We always accuse others of profiting unjustly from our labor yet we work and dismiss our long hours in the fields. We're resigned to our fates, we're reluctant to take advantage of benefits, we play stupid, but I'm not—I went to

UNAM, the National Autonomous University of Mexico, and graduated with a masters in economics. I never say it because it doesn't mean anything here. You all complain about your low wages yet you've never asked for a pay raise."

Carmen was amazed by Christina's admission but the conversation returned to its meaningless chatter.

"Did you read in the paper, someone found the bones of Jesus?" Karina asked.

"That tortilla image of Christ sold for a thousand dollars," Dolores quipped.

"I wonder if it was His bones as a boy or man," Karina wondered.

"I can't do it, Carmen. I don't have papers, they'll send me back," Refugia said as she kneaded masa, rolled out the dough.

"Me too, I can't," Martina added.

An older woman said, "It won't work, once a Mexican makes it, they turn against their own kind."

Nestora sighed, "It's true, a Mexican gets a green card and they think they're higher, the elite of migrants whose backs the INS dried out with nice soft towels. They're no longer *mojados*. Reminds me of the song, 'La Jaula de Oro,' the line that goes *even though the cage is golden, it is still a prison.*"

Carmen cut in, "We're not going to march or protest, just file a grievance and present it to Mr. Miller. It's not going to get you deported or lose you your job."

"If we organize a committee, they'll mark us as troublemakers. It's a waste, it'll change nothing."

★   ★   ★

Later that evening, after she and Lorenzo had finished washing his pickup, she leaned against the truck grill.

"Come on, the keys," he demanded.

"Come get them." She clenched them between her teeth, lay across the hood, and gave a deep husky laugh.

"You look like a fish with a hook in your mouth," he said. "Keys." He extended his hand for them.

"Come get them," she mumbled.

In an instant he was on the hood and had her in his arms. Coming out of the kiss he had the keys in his mouth.

"That's how you get the keys to a woman's heart," he said.

"That's how you reel a fish in," she countered, teasing. She had been at the camp just short of a year now and she had no doubt her future would be with Lorenzo.

22

March 2002

Vito reassured Rafael that his business with Puro was strictly boxing and he promised it would stay that way. He had no inclination to sell drugs or get involved in any of Puro's criminal activities. Rafael begrudgingly assented to the boxing. Rafael knew from having a brother who had been a boxer that if boxing was in the blood, no power in the world could keep the fighter from entering the ring.

They stayed up and talked a little, ate beans and rice. Vito decided to sleep outside in the truck bed, under the stars, to be alone. Rafael went to bed and didn't tell him about his father's stroke.

Vito thought, snuggling in the sleeping bag in the back of his pickup, that all the rich Puros in the world couldn't own the stars. His legs were sore, his face ached, and his mind was still swimming with images of the fight. Shifting his head on the gym bag he was using as a pillow, he saw himself walking from the back of the cantina where the fight had been, gloves dangling over his shoulder, leather laces rubbing his neck. It was the first time people had stood and nodded at him with respect.

April 2003

The match with Stud a year back had been one in a series of incidents that ignited the divine plan of his life. First, his father had put him on the scraper. Then he had whipped the grower's kid who had insulted Carmen and been thrown out of camp. The pipes had crashed through Puro's Escalade window; his boxer had canceled and Vito had agreed to pay for the damages by taking his place.

He breathed deeply, inhaled the night air. He was amazed that his life consisted of a patchwork of coincidences—nothing planned or merited, his life was as unpredictable as it was satisfying, especially when the ref raised his arm as the winner.

He was becoming familiar with fight fans and it seemed they loved the violence, the drama, and beyond that, cared little about the gladiators in the ring. It was a spectacle or sideshow for them to enjoy.

His growing disaffection for boxing fans, particularly Chicanos and Mexicans, and something about putting his life on the line for what he loved made him feel contempt for those who sat on the sidelines enjoying it. After his first fight and thereafter, for the next nine months and some thirty fights, he nursed a secret repugnance for them.

Vito got serious about training and fought continuously, every three weeks, in warehouses, on flatbed trailers outside of truck stops, at concrete urban basketball courts, in barrio parks, at country bars, on factory floors, and by seaside docks, flattening his opponents as though he were puncturing tires with a knife, deflating the fight in them.

And despite his private disdain for the crowds, he provoked them by shouting, "This fight is for you! For those who sweat to earn their money! Stand up, *mojados,* stand up, Chicanos!"

Even after many fights, he had much to learn. He had the brawling eagerness of a raw, young champion, punches flailing like storm-hurled stones.

He was learning to use the space in the ring like a bird swerves and cuts and swoops through air, and not even his lack of experience culled the mesmerizing luster of his youthful movements, in his gangling swing, his awkward darts, his back and sideways missteps and the way he recovered his balance, dodging in those vulnerable pockets of insecurity and fear glinted the sparkle of a deeper source of blinding power, destructive and avenging, shimmering now like a mirror that catches the sunlight and flashes reflections of brilliant rays awakening to its destiny.

After every fight, Vito collapsed in bed aching and lay on his back, inhaling hard to catch his breath as the spinning in his head slowed and he gradually recovered his sensibilities, deeply fulfilled. He dreamed fights, tossing and turning with opponents.

He went to parties with barbecue and beer—lighthearted, festive celebrations. He was becoming the people's hero. There were bonfires with women and children gathered around telling stories about his fights, his unequalled bravery and mythical strength. There were those who composed *corridos* and sang about him, strumming guitars. At every gathering, there was a plank set across two fifty-gallon drums and amid the old cars, broken washing machine, bricks, sinks, and splintered benches, flood lamps rigged to the horizontal bar of a swing set without swings lit up a decapitated goat hanging upside down as its blood drained into zinc buckets. Men took shifts turning the homemade barrel roasters as chili seeds popped in the butane roasting cylinders. The freshly butchered goat meat was cooked over fire on spits and all the while people deferred to Vito, clapping for him, patting his back, and crying "El Campeon!" He washed the chili and goat down with tequila.

He'd hang out with the people just long enough to show his gratitude for the food, the same ones who cheered with satisfaction when he almost lost. Everybody loved seeing an upcoming contender win, but losing quenched their appetites, too. He knew that, like all people forming relationships, his fans were two-blooded—lose and they went cold and indifferent, keep winning and they'd sacrifice their lives for you. People were fickle, especially those falling in love with another person. People loved boxers and as long as a boxer won he could do anything he wanted. However, if he lost, he could be the pope's brother and they'd hate him.

Because his parents were Mexican immigrants, the Mexicans adored him. And because he and his brother Lorenzo were Chicanos, born on this side of the border, the Americans loved him.

He talked loudly and brazenly, didn't care what others thought and had no interest in social propriety, manners, and sweet appearances. He did without the niceties but harassed fans rooting for the opponent, aggravated them when they booed him, incited spectators with derisive antics in the ring, egging them on with obscene slurs and gestures. He didn't care because he knew that the first time he lost they'd be on him like a pack of hyenas on a freshly gutted carcass.

Their contradictions annoyed him and it was not his nature to philosophize; he went straight to the mark. They would never file a grievance on their own behalf, yet they whined about their suffering. Patriotic to a fault and proven a thousand times in battle, they'd throw themselves on a grenade to save others, yet were fearful of complaining to the boss about their low wages.

He despised the "I'll do whatever you want me to do" part of them, the "I'll work no matter how you treat me," "I'll drive myself to death if you want" part of them. He knew how each stood out in the cold waiting for a business owner to drive up and select some of them to work that day. They faithfully observed laws meant to benefit the bosses who stole their labor, stole their hours, and stole their lives away, and yet they taught their children to never steal. He was not like them, he would never beg for a job or be a slave to anyone.

He'd see himself starve before he'd gather with them under the elm tree at dawn, drinking coffee, laughing at the mishaps of others, swearing to the truth of their half-true stories, lying about how their scars happened, rehashing their journeys with terrifying escapes and point-blank near-deaths, telling how they'd been robbed by thieves and swindled by friends, how new acquaintances proved false, while stamping cold from their work boots, their eyes shiny with the day's promise that they might be hired on, eager to work as someone's slave.

Vito scorned their martyrdom, their playing naive and powerless spectators to their own suffering. Hustlers stacked the deck, shuffled and reshuffled and cut, then dealt each a sucker's hand, and each lost until they had nothing left but their sweaty T-shirt and muddy boots. Field rows offered nothing but the joker's card; the peppers and leaves scoffed at their stupidity, each card in the marked deck ridiculed their lives, chuckled and mocked their wretchedness.

23

February 2004

The curse had followed Casimiro all these years, the accidental bullet fired from the chamber was packed with the gunpowder of his dreams when it ripped through the man's suit, punctured his flesh, shattered bone, and pummeled into the heart meat. The bullet killed his own hope to live a life with integrity. It cursed every breath and every act from that point on.

Yes, the curse's jarring hum droned within every thought, as now, thinking of himself as a hypocrite for going along with Miller to send Vito away two years back, when he, Casimiro, was guilty of much worse.

Nothing could lessen the menace that haunted his sleep each evening, tightening the curse-vise one more turn on his bones. He spit when he felt its kiss grinding on his lips. It gripped him with such gloom that not even the river breeze shaking pheasants from the river grass could blow it away. All he could do now was stare at the water, blame himself as he felt the curse oozing from his pores.

I'll go away he had said at the time, almost twenty-five years ago, but the crime returned with an intensity that grew ever more harrowing. He was fifteen when the man from Mexico City arrived one day on his porch. He had an air of gentrified leisure, holding an alligator-skin briefcase, wearing a dark suit with a white shirt, blue suspenders, and ankle-high black boots.

His politeness belied his intent. Casimiro overheard the man talking to his parents at the door. He informed them that he had been sent from the mortgage company in Chihuahua to collect five months' back payments or they'd have to repossess the house. His father had borrowed money from the mortgage company promising to make full payment within three years and the note was now due.

That evening was the first time Casimiro had ever seen his father cry—head down, moaning and broken. He regretted borrowing the money and blamed his predicament on the owners who had closed the coalmine months ago and put him out of work. That night he heard his mother praying behind the bedroom door, pleading with God to save their home.

That a stranger could arrive and take their house seemed impossible. Doesn't he know Papa's been looking for work? That he's been taking anything he can find?

The next morning, Casimiro found the man in his hotel room enjoying room service. "Here's some of the money," he said, extending his hand and an envelope with the money he had saved up for years.

The man humored the boy. "Well, let's see what you have." The man gave a chuckle, dabbed his mouth with the napkin stuffed in his collar, and motioned his hand at him, "Come."

He looked in the envelope and said, "This is very honorable of you, son. Looks like about ten dollars and change. It's an admirable gesture and you probably did this on your own. But there is nothing I can do. It is a lot of money your parents owe and my hands are tied. I was only sent to handle this. *I'm* not taking your house, the mortgage company is, for a loan your father took out against the house. He has not paid it back. You don't understand the situation, and I'm sorry, but you must go now."

But Casimiro did not budge.

The man wiped his hands and considered the situation while fingering his tobacco pipe that had sat on the table next to a dish with a half grapefruit. He felt threatened by the boy now and, thinking the boy might try to harm him, he demanded, "Out!"

Casimiro ordered his feet to move and his body to follow, and perhaps it was shock but he was paralyzed and couldn't do anything but stare at the man, who suddenly reached out and seized him by the shirt.

"Now, out!" Bits of fried egg speckled his lips.

"But you can't take our house, it's ours," was all he could manage to say.

"It's not my doing, I simply work for the mortgage company and I have my instructions." He stood up from the table. "Now, out!" and he shoved him into the hallway and closed the door.

Casimiro stumbled out the hotel door and into the street. He was shaken and dazed by the confrontation and needed to calm down.

He decided to visit Concha, the old crone who sold cheap corn whiskey to anyone. After drinking more than he should have, he roamed aimlessly in the streets and within the hour found himself back at the man's door, opening it without knocking. The room smelled of cologne and tobacco smoke. The room-service cart was gone and the man had changed clothes and now wore a green suit that shimmered like silk with the light shining through the window; his briefcase lay open on the bed and he was arranging papers, banknotes, and pesos.

He turned when he heard the door, reached inside his jacket, and pulled a revolver from his breast pocket. "I thought I told you to go away." Their eyes narrowed on each other and Casimiro lunged at the man.

He didn't know what else to do, it was pure instinct and self-defense and he was just as alarmed as the man was.

The man knocked Casimiro down with the pistol and Casimiro curled up on the floor to protect himself from the kicks and slaps to his shoulders and face. "I warned you. You think I'm someone to toy with?"

Casimiro sprang up, feeling a surge of violence arise in him, and clutched the man's neck, squeezed his thumb and middle finger into the man's throat until his mouth drooled foam. The man's face turned red and his eyes bulged as he clawed at Casimiro. Then he raised the gun.

They wrestled and Casimiro didn't remember ever touching the pistol but there was a loud report that made his ears ring, followed by an absence of sound. The man gulped for air, swirled the huge orbs of his terrified eyes around the room, and collapsed.

Casimiro never told anyone about this incident but, as though by divine retribution, a poultry virus struck the village and wiped out half its inhabitants, including his parents. Infected houses were burned and soon after the last of the victims were buried, he left the village before authorities could arrive from Mexico City and investigate the murder.

It was hard for him to think the word "murder," much less admit that he had committed such a horrendous crime. But he was an accursed murderer and he was convinced that those he loved had been taken away from him as the result of that evil brand. He never understood how so many things could be affected by one dishonorable act.

Sitting under a tree in his wheelchair, gazing at Lorenzo in his worn jeans and a patched plaid shirt as he walked down the row, urging pickers to pick up the pace, Casimiro recalled how in the summer they would plant their own little garden behind the Pullman car. The joy in his son's eyes when Lorenzo pulled up his first onion and first radish had made an impression that had fossilized in his heart. The same thing had happened when he would fill the livestock trough with water and watch his sons splash giddily inside it for hours.

And despite the fact that when Lorenzo was born they had no running water or electricity, and although they boiled their drinking water and never dreamed of a pediatrician visit or immunization shots, they were all healthy and happy.

Casimiro's heart smiled now as he remembered how Lorenzo had called Nopal's breast Nanu, and how, with a ferocious appetite, he'd muster up all his energy to suckle every last drop of milk and frighten yard chickens from woodpiles and scatter prairie doves from trees as he cried, "Nanu! Nanu! Nanu!" content only when he was nuzzled up against Nopal's warm breast, guzzling at the nipple.

Nopal had sung Lorenzo to sleep, composing songs about his first smile, first rollover, first step, first time he said ma ma, her husky-hot voice in his own head now like thunder in the mountains.

Lorenzo was now a man but still doing the same old thing as when he was a small boy, in the rows around the plants. At the end of these rows were more rows and more rows, a labyrinth that would never free them. The rows went on forever, taking them deeper; every row picked turned into miles of rows unpicked.

Casimiro dozed off and woke confused, the reality beyond his eyes fuzzy as he slowly emerged from the depths of his dream, surprised to find himself sprawled on the ground on his back, humiliated when he noticed he had peed his pants. How could he live like this? Constantly needing the help of others to perform the simplest tasks, a decrepit invalid, even a toddler could work more than he could. It was because of the curse that he could no longer rely on his two feet.

With his good left hand he hit the ground repeatedly, wishing only to get up. He rolled in the dirt like a demented animal shot through the head, groaning in shame, cursing with humiliation, his good hand clawing the ground, blowing through his nostrils to clear a circle of sand as he grunted, unable to move, on the ground. For the first time he truly wished for death; it would be better than enduring this disgraceful groveling.

Two hours later, workers rescued him and set him back in his wheelchair. As he watched them return to work, he thought of the thousands over the past sixteen years who had worked in these fields and he promised himself that before his own body devoured him, he would see his son free of the rows.

24

September 1983

Nopal had a dream on the morning of her fifteenth birthday, a dream so powerful it woke her and made her sit up in bed. She listened to the bells from the Guadalajara cathedral next to the *mercado* where she worked selling huaraches. They rang at 5:00 a.m. and woke her parents, who were downstairs shuffling around in the kitchen. She snuggled under the blankets again and slowly spiraled back into sleep.

The dream reflected what was happening in reality. In it, she saw drug lords confiscate peasant lands, forcing the poor who remained to cultivate coca plants and poppies for heroin. The homeless were everywhere. Thousands poured into the city, toting bed-sheet bundles containing all they owned. They huddled on sidewalks and under freeway overpasses, curled on park benches, clustered in alleys, and grouped in rag and cardboard settlements in tree groves, sewer ravines, and run-off culverts. The beaten down, the hopeless, and the elderly begged at intersections as the young were kidnapped and sold as sex slaves in broad daylight.

When she woke from the dream she did what she had been planning to do. She wrote a note to her parents, telling them not to worry and that she loved them. She took the money she had saved for two years selling sandals in the market, packed a few clothes in her backpack, slung her guitar over her back, and left.

She loved and hated Mexico, she thought, as she walked her normal route through the city of bells. Part of her was sad to leave her beautiful city, which boasted more cathedrals, churches, and chapels than any other city in the world, and yet she was happy that she was finally going *pa'l norte*.

As if bidding her good-bye, the bells rocked the cobblestones beneath her leather shoes and rippled up her thighs. She smiled at newlyweds exiting chapels holding hands, rice and flower petals raining on them. Couples strolled and others lounged on benches, buying flowers from vendors and posing for photographers. Some lingered on cathedral steps waiting their turn before the priest.

She glimpsed a carnival on a side street, barrios celebrating one of their many holidays. She paused to let it pass—an array of unbelievably skinny horses pulling field carts clip-clopped by. She was amused by the children, some as young as two and three, dressed as scraggly cornstalks, bouncing up and down around their parent's knees—worker children with soiled faces and bodies smeared with coal dust. And then the extraterrestrial creatures: groups of men and women with wire wings towered on stilts above the heads of the spectators, each masked spirit representing good or evil. Masked faces painted in angelic or grotesque features excited the crowd pressing shoulder to shoulder, thronging both sides of the street, until Death appeared—a white-skinned man on hairy cloven-hoofed stilts. Then, the children scattered, screaming and frightened women followed suit. It unsettled Nopal as she watched it all, thinking that maybe it was a bad omen for her trip to the land of whites.

Nopal hurried, moving through a long corridor of palm trees waving good-bye, the breeze whipping the fronds back and forth. She turned a corner and thought how much she would miss the museum. She slowed to peer in the door at the pre-Columbian art and saw and heard the jade jaguar head growl farewell as the turquoise eagle slashed the air with lightning from its alabaster rock wings and the crocodile splashed around obsidian boulders.

She read a plaque beneath one of the statues outside the building: When enough spirits from the departed have entered us, only then will we come to life again and join you.

Farther on, past the art museum, Diego Rivera's and José Clemente Orozco's murals freed themselves from the walls and crowded the doorways, thick-ankled and broad-shouldered women carried bundles of freshly picked lilacs and revolutionaries' machetes waved her luck.

Laborers rode high on cement sacks in the back of pickups; fruit cutters stood on corners; thousands of bicyclists, each carrying two or three riders, streamed by; skinny horses trudged past pulling rickety carts laden with barrels of water or heaps of vegetables; uniformed schoolgirls and schoolboys smiled at her; and the colorful birds in the trees perforated the silence with angelic voices as lush green plants entwined her feet unwilling to let her go, unwilling to release her from the city. A woman's voice floated from an open window and she memorized one line from her song, "You will blunt the blades with your voice."

She would miss these people but they would never really be absent. In the cellar of her heart, a mad angel mixed and brewed them into her songs—sultry and moody songs, calloused and perfumed and smelly, acidic and balmy, they were carried north, *pa'l otro lado,* with her backpack and guitar.

And as she walked, she thought of America and she felt a new language of hope birthing in her, she sensed a freedom within reach, to reshape her life. She was within reach of a dream, which was to sing and play her guitar.

Oh, these people, she thought as she stopped at a sidewalk shack to eat tacos, these people impulsively blowing their week's wages on binges, partying on the truck tailgates under trees, blasting *corridos,* all proud in new jeans, boots, pearl-button western shirts, and leather belts stamped with MEXICO in green, red, and white, strutting about as the finest specimen of man on earth. They pocket the vows they muttered on their knees before home altars and, prayers forgotten, they drink—everyone understands why, enjoy it, laugh with them—they are not disrespected and when they pass out, friends carry them to bed.

She was drawn to them as the tongue and breath to the harmonica reed, drawn to their genuine love for life, their common sense, their desire to avoid trouble, their haughtiness, and their timid contempt for the privileged.

She would dream her new life into existence and the Mexicans and Chicanos of the north would teach her to trust fate and counsel her about how spirits bless you and how you must listen and follow and believe. Yes, she knew her songs would come from below, from the molten blood-lake of singers from ancient Mayas to Incas to Aztecs to Mexicans to present-day Chicanos, all believing that nurturing one pearl of dignity, planting one corn-seed of hope, sunning one flower-seed of love was more longed for than all the power and money in the world.

She desired to know and name and call forth from lyrics a self-respect she had never known but could taste like fire on her tongue. She would learn to sing for the sullen ones, for the ones who don't talk, for the ones who are nervous and listless and indifferent and pretend not to hurt, for the spiritual ancestors and the spirits of trees and earth and water and air.

And as she walked toward the train station, lightning danced in her heart, giving her journey north an epic energy, a certainty of knowing what to say, how to feel, where to kneel and sleep and stand. She'd witness those with power—a perpetual air of patience about them—break down, weeping on their knees; she'd see passive ones strike out violently; she'd encounter in those who roamed the desert, cruel brutalities and lovely kindness existing side by side. She would not shame what was hidden in one's heart, but turn regret into acceptance and reconnect their breathing to that which had once brought them close to God.

A voice in her heart sang above the death cough of a cat-fish in a dry ditch, it belted out above pain, singing beyond it, blind to the fire in her joints. And if blood were to pour through her ears and nose, she'd let it pour because she had work to do, rows to pick, plants to cut; she had to keep the hoeing going and the singing hot. If the body gives up, goes down, can't stand, there is still work to do, chores to attend, mending and bending and walking and carrying, and she would celebrate it all in song.

That's what her heart told her as she reached the train station and hopped a cattle train with other Mexicans going north to America. And it kept telling her that, into the next evening, when she was already halfway to the border and the train stopped at a cattle yard in a small town and a man jumped into the boxcar.

He sat by her, said he was from Culiacán, and he seemed friendly enough. They exchanged a few words sitting next to each other and then he stood by the open cattle-car door adjusting himself and brooding on the passing landscape until darkness fell. Nopal was exhausted and she dozed off but was startled awake with a gasp.

The man was on top of her, grabbing her breasts, groping between her legs. The other Mexicans in the car looked on, afraid to get involved. The man was holding her down, his hand over her mouth. She felt the predator's lust in his grip when he yanked her head back and slugged her. He knotted her hair around his fist and dragged her back so quickly and with such force she didn't know what was happening.

Her survival instinct kicked in and she bit him, tearing a chunk of flesh from his ribs. He hissed that after fucking her, he would gut her. He snapped the button of her jeans, slid her pants down, and opened her legs.

She clawed his arms and face, bit his hand, feeling cheap as his fingers poked inside her. He kept hitting her but she kept squirming; he slammed his knee into her jaw and lunged on top of her to dominate her. She felt like a flea caught in the mouth of an erupting volcano.

Then Nopal freed one of her arms, grabbed the knife stashed in her boot, and in one clean stroke, starting at his testicles and slashing up, she cut him between his legs.

He fell over and howled in horror.

Nopal scrambled to her feet. The other men in the car grouped together and moved toward her, ordering her to jump or they'd push her off. She grabbed her backpack and guitar case, threw them first, and then leaped, rolling over and over in the dirt and weeds. The last thing she heard as the moving train sped forward was the man screaming, "You'll pay for this, you whore!"

She spent the night hiding in creosote bushes, the brutality of the rape running over and over in her head. She was in disbelief. Looking out at nothing, unaware that she was raking her fingers repeatedly through her hair, she became filled with a deep sense of gloom that God had abandoned her. The image of the man slapping her returned. She raised her arms to protect herself, turned her face away from the hurt, and then because conscious that it was only memory. *Only memory,* she repeated, as she touched her swollen lip, felt the still-moist red stains of blood on her jeans over her thighs, crotch, and stomach.

She wiped the knife blade with some leaves and stuffed it back in her boot. She scrubbed her hands with dirt to clean away the blood but it wouldn't come off.

How could such violence have happened? Her eyes searched for answers in the stars in the sky, in the firm soil under her boots, in the moon above earth, in the millions of other galaxies beyond our universe—why, why did this man board the cattle car and attempt to rape her? Why didn't the others try to help?

She had given no provocation, in fact, her jeans, T-shirt, and jacket were loose and masculine looking. Besides an exchange of a few, brief words, she hadn't looked at him, hadn't talked to him or engaged his attention in any way.

The violation chilled her. A scream of denial thickened in her throat but never came. Instead, tears streamed from her eyes, eyes that felt loose in their bone sockets, like they might fall out of her face. She felt like her body didn't belong to her anymore.

Her fingers wanted to free themselves from her hands and crawl into the weeds. Her right ear was torn and bleeding and felt like it might fly away. Her feet were anvils, bruised from the hammering she had endured as the man twisted and stomped them.

She touched the parts of her body that hurt and ached and drew her knees up to her chin and rested her head on them. After a while, she wheezed her tears out and started pounding her forehead against her knees to feel pain, to claim her body again.

After a long time she got up and walked a couple of hours into the night until she came to a small town. She washed at a gas station, changed in the bathroom into clean clothes, and threw the bloody clothing into a Dumpster.

As the sun rose over the horizon, it was a normal morning, cars appeared and pedestrians filled sidewalks on their way to their jobs. Nopal promptly went to the train yard and, within the hour, jumped on another cattle car and resumed her journey north.

Part Three

25

June 2005

North of the fields and a little beyond the camp, where half a dozen migrant trailers and shacks circled the compound, three warehouse flood lamps threw nets of light misted by flying insects. They illuminated the weary tractors parked by every warehouse door.

Tractors have much more to them than a city person might think.

Lorenzo knew a tractor was a tool, but to make it yield something took common sense and life experience, belief in something beyond Lorenzo's own strength and effort. When Lorenzo turned the key, it was to make money to feed and care for his father and other families in need. Just as the plants were more than plants, more than the cutting and pulling of peppers off the stems—there was the seed, and before that, preparing the soil, and before that, Lorenzo standing in the middle of a nondescript piece of dirt, looking at the stars and breathing in, praying this crazy idea of water, seed, and earth could make him a living.

It was summer, and because it was a bumper crop harvest, Lorenzo hired a dozen additional field-workers. Their cars around the camp, by the river trailers and alongside the field rows, seldom moved once they were parked; they were the migrants' temporary homes.

Then there were the college kids, volunteering until the end of August, at which point their research papers on the environment or labor or sustainable communities would be done and they'd head back to school for fall. Migrant cars and trucks were rusty and dirty; the students' vehicles were tattooed with activist stickers advocating one green cause or another. The last few would be gone by the end of the picking season, when September turned the chili from green to red and early October stripped yellowing leaves off stems, ditch water dried up, cranes and geese scattered south, and the earth chilled.

Dimitri, who had been one of the college volunteers in the fields a few years before, now turned off the interstate toward the camp. Lorenzo had contacted him and they had started seeing each other regularly. An hour ago, Dimitri had gotten off an airplane in El Paso and rented a car. Now the bright moon shining over the quiet fields reminded him of the good old days. Irrigation water trickled in furrows and, from stalwart roots, peppers whispered their plans to the sun.

A coyote barked somewhere in the hills east of the highway. Dimitri rolled his window down and the constant *swoosh-swoosh* of vehicles going ninety on the interstate blew cool air over his face and refreshed him as he turned right, down the dirt road running beside the field. His headlights aimed over the fields, illuminating to the far side of the river where the air was thick with flying insects.

Lorenzo saw him approaching, headlights bobbing up and down. Dimitri was not coming to work in the fields as he had when they first met and he was a freshman at a private New York college; he was here to deliver three hundred thousand dollars.

They gave each other a light embrace and Dimitri handed him the army duffel bag. Lorenzo took it into the warehouse, to a backroom, and emptied the cash out onto a table and started counting it.

"I thought I taught you how to fight," Lorenzo stated as he counted the hundreds and bundled them with rubber bands in ten-thousand-dollar stacks.

"What are you talking about?"

"The scratches."

"Oh, my neck, you wouldn't believe it."

"A little love spat?"

"Last night I was in a bar in Brooklyn, you know, talking to this guy, bought him a beer, killing time, and I tell him that I'm flying to New Mexico today to see an old friend—" Dimitri's face turned red. "Fucking neo-Nazi."

Lorenzo looked up but kept counting. "What'd he say?"

"I guess he thinks this is still Mexico. He started in about Mexicans taking jobs, abusing the system."

"Seriously? So you popped him?"

"Well, I let him go on a while but then he said we should round up all the Mexicans in a corral and shoot them—that's when I popped him and the little bitch scratched me. A white Nationalist, that's what he was."

"He was a little bitch scratcher," Lorenzo said and Dimitri laughed.

"Now he's not talking to anyone, I tell you that. I got him good."

"So Mr. Ivy Leaguer, do you think Mexicans are going to take all your daddy's law firm money?"

"Man, don't play that on me, man. It's serious. Punk starts talking shit about swarming hordes, animal-like people, public health risk, raping white girls."

Lorenzo finished counting the money and they went outside and sat on a bench under a cottonwood. They shared a joint.

"Chalk one up for the Ivy Leaguers."

They both smiled, nodding as they gazed over the fields.

"And what's up with Vito? They still got him kicked out or what?"

"Yup. It was the middle of 2002, now it's '05, almost three years."

"I liked that dude. He was crazy in a good way, used to liven things up around here."

"Yeah, that's my brother. You were just this gangly long-haired college kid carrying a grungy backpack and a skateboard with all those antiwar slogan stickers, and when you emptied the backpack, I'll never forget—"

"Out fell packs of green tea, vitamins, flax seed, a beat-up journal. Blah blah blah."

"Man," Lorenzo smiled, "least you weren't one of those fraternity kids we get sometimes, suited more for black-tie banquets than dirty work."

"I agree." He paused, "But look who's talking."

"What do you mean?"

"Didn't you say something about this chick from the university, San Diego?"

"Ah man, it's getting serious. I gave her a ring."

"What? You didn't tell me! Damn, that's crazy. Congratulations! How long you two been going together?"

"Two years. She got here when Vito got kicked out. Hell, it took me about six months to ask her out, another six to ask her to be my girlfriend. Thank god, I'm making a little money. It takes money to be in love."

"She's doing all this? Used to be nothing but dirt fields, now it looks like a soccer field and educational buildings of some type."

"That's what they are. We hired tutors and teachers, bought books and computers for the workers and their kids. We have a soccer team now."

"And you used to scoff at money, say it was evil and that the rich were the scourge of the planet. Now, my good friend, you believe me when I say it can be put to good use."

They each took another toke.

Dimitri looked around. "Ah, I see you're liking it a little too much. New truck, watch, expensive boots. It can be very addictive."

"I blow a lot of it on Carmen. We spent a weekend in El Paso, stayed in a sweet little place, went out and ate, drank, you know . . . talked a lot."

"Yeah right, talked." They laughed.

"No, serious. We're talking about a life together. We even drove up north to southern Colorado and I did all this crazy shit."

"Like?"

"I actually shopped for fruit and vegetables at a health food store. That was weird. I mean, I picked it all my life and then I'm buying it with all these health nuts."

"I know the kind, they look like my mom. You know, some things in life are inevitable, and change is one of them. That's what makes it sweet; we can never predict change. That was some good weed. Never had it so fine. I've given them names and my clients love it—purple butterfly, powdered cocoon, crystalline resin, phosphorescent black, scintillating green." Dimitri narrowed his lips and whistled. "Worth its weight in gold."

"I'll have another load in two weeks."

Starting in July 2004, almost a year before, with money coming in, Carmen and Lorenzo had upgraded the camp. Four new pod buildings were added, tutors were hired, and after-school programs in music, karate, and boxing were set up. They bought a dozen goats and began their own herd then started a plant and child nursery run by the older female pickers. Young men were apprenticed to older ones who taught them carpentry and they made desks, furniture, and cabinets. Electricians, plumbers, and masons took young ones under their wings and taught them the trades.

It didn't bother Carmen that it was profit from selling marijuana that made life better. Marijuana, Carmen reasoned, was a gift from mother earth and throughout her life she'd known so many people who smoked it and were nice people that she had no qualms about Lorenzo selling it. She was, however, against hard drugs of any kind—she loathed meth, cocaine, heroin, and crack, and felt deeply sad for the addicts whose lives were being destroyed by them.

Miller never suspected where the money was coming from and as far as he was concerned, he believed Carmen when she said she had applied for grants and gotten them for the expanded human services now offered at the camp.

A sense of fullness and good fortune permeated the days at the camp and it made Carmen feel grounded enough to start making plans for herself and Lorenzo.

They drove to San Diego to meet her parents and break the news that they were engaged. During that week, while they picnicked at the zoo and dined at the marina on a ship docked in the bay, Carmen's mother worried for her daughter's future. She hadn't exactly dreamed of her ending up as a chili picker's wife. She suggested Lorenzo attend university and study agriculture. She was afraid of prying too deep, fearful he might respond by telling her they were going to live in a jungle or on a reservation. Her father, on the other hand, was fine with Lorenzo and, though he didn't talk much, he kept telling Carmen's mother, "He's a good man. You watch, he'll be someone, he'll be someone."

Lorenzo and Carmen managed to break away to spend an evening at the theater enjoying a modern jazz dance troupe. Another night they strolled along the sea, watching the pelicans and seagulls on the shore as the waves ebbed and flowed, kissing as the setting sun lowered.

The last day of their visit he gave Carmen's parents his mother's green chili recipe, telling them that it went great with an egg and potato breakfast. Lorenzo promised that when they came to visit he'd take them rabbit hunting and fishing.

26

January 2005

Vito was back in Albuquerque and when he walked into the barbershop after being absent almost two and a half years, there were the same faces sitting in the same chairs, watching the same sports channel. When they turned and saw him, their eyes glinted hard and sharp. It was clear there had been many rumors about the reason for his disappearance.

"When'd you get out?" one guy asked.

"Was never in," Vito replied and added, looking up at the boxers on TV, "that's bullshit, he can't fight. I whipped him in the Amarillo stockyards—punked his ass."

"Heard you was running from the law," another man offered.

Vito's hair was long, his clothes smelled of too many nights on the road sleeping in his truck. "None of it's true, I split off from Rafael for a while."

Two and half years ago, at the end of 2002, he had taken off with Ronny, a big Déné Indian, and together they'd been to every reservation west of the Mississippi in at least fifty matches—in community centers, auditoriums, bars, VFW halls, bowling alleys, abandoned warehouses, hotels, parks, and county fairs; they had even done cage fighting and corral wrestling. There was no such thing as a draw—the rule was simple, one man walks out of the ring. Five or twelve or twenty rounds, until one went down. No headlines or sports-page write-ups; the fights were arranged in backrooms over cigars and whiskey.

Vito didn't care who they were—Chicanos, Asians, or Gringos, they all hit the concrete, the dirt, or the canvas, and though it wasn't a million-dollar purse, he had enough pocket change, after splitting it with his road-dog Ronny, to satisfy his meager needs—a good meal, a woman, and a warm bed.

"You see," he said, sitting down, "used to be old schoolers believed fighters get in a ring to fight. None of that dancing and dodging as if they were rehearsing on stage for a ballet." He paused, "I beat him," he said again.

The men turned their eyes from the television to Vito, mulled over his lie.

"It's not on record," Vito added.

A thoughtful silence followed this statement.

Then one man growled, "I lost money on you. You were supposed to fight and you didn't show."

"Ask Puro how much of my earnings he stole from me. How many of you are willing to work without getting paid?"

They were Puro's friends and a silence stretched out tense as a slingshot until the barber tapped the chair for Vito. "You look worse than a goat."

"De-lice him," one joked. "So, where you been?"

"You wouldn't believe it," Vito said and started to tell the tale.

Vito whipped a big Indian at the Grants, New Mexico, powwow and on his way to the next fight he had dropped in at a Navajo bar by Jemez Pueblo and bought drinks for the whole bar. A one-armed Indian slid in next to him at the bar and told him that the Indians in suits worked for the Bureau of Indian Affairs and were no good. Knowing nothing about the BIA, Vito denounced them as traitors, warning them not to drink the tequila shots. He went along the counter taking their drinks away until Ronny slammed him in the face and all hell broke loose. It was a good fight but then Vito knocked Ronny down and carried him out the back door.

They shook their heads in amazement and murmured, "Oh, it's a crazy world out there."

Someone else now opined, "You get some of the Indians drunk and you've got real problems on your hands."

Vito agreed and after his haircut, all clean and smelling of talcum powder and hair tonic, he headed to the junkyard on the outskirts of the city.

Rafael and a few workers were up on the scaffold against the north wall, laying bricks. When Rafael turned, he saw a piece of plywood stacked high with bricks. He didn't know who was under it, but spoke a warning.

"You have pride in your strength now but your back will pay the bill later."

"I can carry ten times as much."

Rafael knew the voice and he steadied himself as the strong hands and arms below set the plywood down. The face of Vito looked up at him.

"*Que voy, tío*," Vito said and smiled.

Rafael climbed down and walked under the portal along the *colonia*—the series of apartments connected with construction scraps he had scavenged from job sites. They sat on a bench. Rafael poured them coffee from his thermos and then sipped.

"I make use of everything: bricks, lumber, wiring, odds, and ends."

Nearby some workers gathered around an oil drum crackling with kindling and as they warmed themselves they smoked and drank coffee.

Rafael had no expression on his face but as he spoke the solemn tone of his voice told it all.

"I didn't tell you, but my brother was a fighter. I trained and managed him. He was ranked in the top ten. He died while jogging, a heart attack. I made a promise to *la Virgen* that I would never get in the fight game again. But I'm telling you, you kicked some serious ass that night."

"Yeah, well, I've caused a lot of trouble for everyone, even my dad. His stroke was probably because he worried so much about me." And after a pause he added, "And my mom, too, her death was probably my fault in some way."

"They're taking good care of him. Your father is fine."

"When can I see him, go back?"

"We'll arrange it soon." Rafael stared at him, trying to answer a question in his mind.

"When I'm beating a man down, there's something so sweet, feeding me something in my soul that gets rid of the pain of living every day."

"So the ring is the only place where you don't fuck things up?" Rafael said.

Vito nodded.

"I said I make use of everything, Vito. I even make use of losers that run away." He put his arm around Vito and patted his shoulder. "*Va esta bien,*" he said.

"And boxing?"

"We'll talk in the morning," Rafael said. "Get something to eat, and get some sleep. Be ready to go at dawn."

27

At four the next morning, even before the sun crested the horizon, they rattled across the prairie, down a dirt road, for an hour, and just after daybreak Rafael finally pulled up in front of an old adobe house. Vito slammed the door of the old homemade welding pickup and Rafael growled at him to take it easy on her. They went down a hill toward a smaller hut with smoke coming out of its chimney. Vito followed him down the winding dirt path, knee-high prairie grass and cacti brushing against their legs.

Men started appearing from all sides and women, too. Boys with dogs raced by in the nearby woods. They walked passed a kiva, then a well-worn ceremonial plaza and open-air stands with signs advertising Chicano food, snow cones, mutton, and chili. The moon illuminated a whitewashed adobe church with stained-glass windows etched with brown saints. Vito had never seen anything like it: one of the windows had an indigenous Virgen de Guadalupe. They came up to a few houses. Chickens scattered and dogs raced beside bumpers of arriving trucks.

A man came out and embraced Rafael in such a rough but intimate way that Vito knew they were old friends. The sun was shining on their faces and crows scattered from trees. Rafael signaled Vito to wait and the two old friends walked over to a lean-to with a blackened *horno,* an outdoor oven, for cooking mutton and fry bread and drying chili. Next to it was a stack of piñon wood. Blue corn dried on the rooftop and red chili *ristras* dangled from vigas and *latillas*.

Another man came up to them. To Vito he seemed important, dressed as he was in white leather pants with a red and blue wool belt and black moccasins with white beads. The three spoke, then nodded for Vito to come and all of them walked back to the house on the hill, Vito following at a distance.

All kinds of people filled the house now and the living room was jammed with grandfathers and grandkids on the couches, talking. Some people held small drums, others rattle gourds; adults laughed at infants trying to dance; pots of red chili, green chili stew, fried potatoes, pinto beans and tortillas, deer, and elk meat simmered on the woodstove. On the walls were pictures of Christ, the brown madonna, Santo Niño de Atocha, and indigenous carved wooden statues representing fire and thunder spirits and season spirits called kachinas.

Vito helped himself to triple servings of corn, barbecue lamb ribs, pinto beans, potato salad, and green chili stew. Then he joined the group of men leaving and they crossed a cornfield, then followed a ravine to a grove of cottonwoods that surrounded a teepee in a grassy clearing where another group of men talked around a bonfire. Horses whinnied from corrals hidden in the trees where mangy barrio dogs darted in and out of the shadows.

The men stripped down to their boxers, piling clothes and shoes on the grass. They became solemn as an older carnal joined them, stood at the fire, and prayed. Then the men bowed and turned to the four directions and followed each other into the teepee.

A pit of hot volcanic rocks burned deep red in the center. Rafael sat across from Vito in the circle and stared right through him, more serious than Vito had ever seen him. He was a different man. The prayer leader signaled for more rocks and as the assistant, the fire keeper, carried them in with a shovel, the prayer leader clacked sacred sticks together and began to hum.

Flames flared wildly and the fire popped and sparked and flashed and leaped between Vito and Rafael. The prayer leader chanted—he welcomed the elders from the east, south, west, and north, spiritual brothers who had come from different barrios to participate in the magic. He sang not so much to the people inside as to the spirits of his ancestors. The fire keeper entered and fed the fire, entered and fed the fire, until the prayer leader motioned that it was enough.

After each of the elders sang their power song, a zinc pail filled with peyote tea was passed around and each person scooped the ladle and took a drink. Vito looked up over the dancing flames at Rafael, who nodded, and Vito dipped the ladle in the pail five times and drank heartily. The rest of the carnals drank only two scoops, and their eyes assessed him, measuring him as one warrior might another. Rafael looked at Vito fully, taking him in, until his brown eyes brimmed with his image and Vito could discern nothing in the look except a familiar but distant intelligence that was both cosmic and earthly. The tea was bitter and grainy with sand. By the time the pail had been passed around the circle a few times,

Vito was well on his way to meeting the spirit animal that had protected and watched over him all these years.

Physical location and the parameters of the day-to-day reality Vito existed in dissolved. Matter blurred into an infinite universe wherein he was soaring high above the mountains, listening to the conversation of the fire. Each flame was an individual dancer, speaking to him in a language he fully understood. The flames made contact with the deepest part of his heart, reconnecting him to events he had already lived but could only now, for the first time, understand.

The fire spoke to him about his father and instructed him how to repair the bridge back to Casimiro's heart. He was bathed in a light, absorbed like a drop of water into a glowing sponge with a million tiny dark holes that led to individual memories of his life. In his mind Vito saw Rafael, worried for him, asking around to everyone about him. He followed Lorenzo and Carmen across the fields where the rest of the migrants were and he hovered above their shoulders as they stooped and cut and carried. Out of the darkness his mother Nopal appeared. She was singing, each word a spark dimly burning in the dark. Suddenly, the volume of her lyrics thundered in his ears and shook the air, shattering his disembodied self into a thousand pieces breathed in by the fiery center of the sun.

Then, only peace.

He found himself lying on his back in a boxing ring in a lush meadow at the foothills of a mountain forested with tall pine trees, the upper half covered in snow. He looked up and did not see stars or sky but hot burning ringlets, halos, millions of them descending all around him. He propped himself up on his elbow, looked around, and saw in his corner his friend from the junkyard whose name he had forgotten. Also in his corner was the father of the boy whose gloves he had found in the trunk of the car. He looked in the opposite direction and saw a fighter standing over him, rage glaring in his eyes, nimble on his toes, eager, on the verge of mauling him.

It was the same face that he had seen when he was a child: it belonged to the man who had walked out of the cantina with his mother through the back door—where they later found her dead, her throat sliced.

It had happened so quickly, the few people smoking cigarettes hardly had time to realize why this woman had shrieked and collapsed. A man kicked at the mongrels licking her blood on the asphalt.

Vito screamed, and then, starting out as a speck in the center of the fire, he grew larger and larger until a shadow silhouette consumed him, fell over him, and sunk into his flesh and he was it—a man standing up with arms spread wide and dancing, dancing, dancing in a ring, boxing gloves raised high.

They came out of the teepee at dawn.

Vito's eyes tracked Rafael as he walked outside to a shed overlooking the prairie, dotted with sheep, to the east. His mind was reeling with what he had heard the fire say in his vision, each word packing a thousand volts of meaning. The fire had talked to him and he was willing to keep it his secret, store it in the back of his mind so he could make choices based on this healing and heart-strengthening experience.

Even as he walked outside the flames from the sacred fire danced before his eyes and filled his mind. A couple of men pulled in with a horse in the back of their truck. It was excited and yanked its head away from the halter rope tethered to the iron rack. The flames obscured them. They hushed Rafael's voice greeting the two Chicano cowboys. Vito turned toward some kids kicking a soccer ball and chasing a goat but he didn't see them. The flames were on them, burning them into vapor and misting the air with the shapes of his mother, father, and brother. His phantom family glanced at him as they made their way down the dirt road, away from the ceremonial teepee.

A breeze carried the scent of his mother's hands rubbing sage together, and the fragrance of cooking smoke made the air as sweet as a fruit orchard. Mexican music came from somewhere. Everything seemed so still, a hovering, glowing stillness, burning through the hardness in his heart, unearthing a trove of memories from the fields—people in camp, his brother's laughter, Carmen's intelligent brown eyes, his father's mysterious look when he searched Vito's face for a sign of maturity, the junkyard and the smell of the sunlight heating up oil and metal and tires and pigeons lined on telephone wires—the flames passing over each image as if it were a magnifying glass, smoldering his emotions to a melancholy regret that made his eyes water.

28

December 2005

It was Friday and a group of field-workers were hanging out in the warehouse, playing poker, waiting for Lorenzo to show up with their checks. As they played they drank beer and talked, worrying about not having work. One of the guys pointed to the warehouse entrance, large enough to drive two tractors through at the same time, and said, "The boss bought that harvesting machine as big as that entrance. It picks up everything and we have to sort through the chili on the belt trying not to get bit by snakes, spiders, and scorpions."

"Those harvesters are taking our jobs."

"If we don't end up in prison first. You've seen what they're doing—building prisons way out in the desert so no one knows they're there."

One man looked up, "I know, I was there. Some bad shit going on. In one day I saw ICE bring in over three hundred immigrants—every day, three hundred are processed, it's gestapo-killing madness, but instead of Jews it's Mexicans. Somewhere out there, there's two thousand immigrants being used for medical experiments, like guinea pigs."

The rest of the men looked at him with skepticism.

"It's not a lie," he insisted. "I've seen those places: no windows, ambulances coming and going with dead people. They have their own buses and vans for transporting prisoners. They put immigrants with criminals and there's rapes, beatings. Poor, poor people in there. They're forbidden to talk, no lawyers are allowed—"

"Can't talk, no?"

"It's the truth! And then the detainees vanish, gone. ICE claims they deport them, but if so, why doesn't anyone see them again? There are no records of the immigrants in those desert prisons, where are they?"

One poker player said, "I'm not sticking around. I'm going farther north after this season, harvest trees in Oregon. The paper industry pays better than this chili crap."

"Cannery for me, in Detroit," said another one. "They give you health insurance, permanent work, no seasonal stuff."

Lorenzo showed up and sat down, handed out checks to the workers, and said, "Deal me in."

He got a good hand and joked, "Since I've taken over my father's job, I'm going to give you paid vacations, health insurance, and I'm going to raise your wages." He was dressed up in a black leather vest, white matador's shirt, leather boots, a gold Movado watch, a silver neck chain with a turquoise cross, and his prized cowboy buckle and black Stetson hat with the snakeskin hatband.

"And I'm a ballerina," the oldest player quipped.

One of the younger players said, "My dad told me that in

the sixties the Brown Berets used to organize the field-workers, they were like Black Panthers, but Chicano. Maybe they can organize us?"

"*Pendejo,* they're not around anymore."

Lorenzo's cell phone rang and he walked away to talk. Another pickup. Outside of Juárez, Mexicans were growing bumper crops of chronic, the best weed in the world. And for Lorenzo, business was booming. He spent every weekend in Juárez and returned late Sunday night; then, weary, eyes hollow, cheeks gaunt, he would unload duffel bags from his pickup and vanish into the back storeroom in the warehouse for hours.

He upgraded his security, bought a safe, installed a hydraulic lift to go up and down the well, and had electronic gadgetry to keep eavesdroppers from listening in on phone calls. Sometimes as many as six customers were lined up in show-room pickups with out-of-state plates behind the warehouse where they loaded up and left quickly, down the dirt road and back to the highway.

29

March 2006

Carmen was industrious and never far from his side, weighing
chili sacks on the truck, boxing produce, rinsing chili, and spraying
down vegetables. When weather forced workers inside and the
soil was so rain-soaked they couldn't step on it without sinking
in to midcalf, when wind ravaged the harvest and scattered leaves
and peppers all over the road and most workers went home, she'd
be typing away on her laptop.

Late at night there'd be a light on in one of the two warehouses and workers knew it was Carmen, doing research and
gathering information from government sites to help improve the
migrant's quality of life.

Carmen cataloged and analyzed the data gathered from the
workers, creating statistical charts of family history, where they
came from, the details of their journey north, general health,
education level, and their culture. In addition to keeping the
personal records of the camp workers, Carmen also kept the
books. Either in the warehouse or under the tree in the compound, Carmen could often be found leaning intently over her
screen and scribbling in her legal pad, tabulating the money

129

coming in from Dimitri and going out to pay the Mexicans who were smuggling the weed in.

Americans had an enormous appetite for good weed. She couldn't believe the demand for it. The marijuana loads were getting bigger and the money was increasingly hard to hide. It was almost as if the camp were a tribe and the migrant workers Indios who shared the gambling proceeds. Lorenzo always found reasons to give small bonuses and each worker appreciated it with his or her silence.

Despite this, the revenue was overflowing and Lorenzo and Carmen had to bury sacks of cash behind the warehouse. But as the volume expanded, so did Carmen's imagination about what to do with the money.

If someone had told her years before about the amount of money that could be made selling a weed that grew from the earth, she would have laughed. But Bible-Belt gringos with bulging briefcases couldn't buy enough of it. African American attorneys from Vegas and Cleveland, and directors and actors from Los Angeles, flew into El Paso and Las Cruces in private jets and loaded up U-Hauls. Out there, beyond the chili rows and the shacks of the migrants, was an unending market of consumers who could purchase more than was possible to supply.

Carmen hired a live-in nurse to care for Casimiro. She hired field-workers to make the Pullman more accommodating, lowering shelves and tables and constructing ramps. She bought a custom wheelchair with special tires for traction so he could wheel to the fields and watch the workers. Once a week, a doctor visited the camp and dispensed medication to him as needed.

Women pointed out her kindness and men commended her, saying their children should do as good a job taking care of them in their old age. Carmen's larger-than-life charity grew to saintly standards one Wednesday afternoon when a new van arrived, fully equipped with the latest technology for the handicapped. By voice command, doors opened, the steering wheel lowered, wiper blades activated, and a hydraulic ramp unfolded to the ground. If there was an emergency, besides the lights going on and the horn blaring, a voice recognition program automatically called 911 and had a satellite system alert authorities to the van's location. And from then on, Carmen was the unrivaled adopted daughter, the one woven into folklore.

Under Carmen's guidance, Lorenzo installed televisions in the warehouse and while women packed boxes for shipment or inspected chili streaming past on the conveyor belts, they listened to their favorite soaps. He hired teachers from the local community college to conduct on-site ESL classes three times a week; he graded a big dirt field into a baseball diamond, chalked it, set up a backstop, bought gloves, balls, and bats, and launched the camp's first baseball team, christened the Little Hot Peppers; he paved a court and installed a basketball net; he bought playground equipment for the kids; and he hired an accountant to teach the workers how to fill out government tax forms, keep books, and budget household expenses.

Consistent with her optimistic outlook, Carmen thought one could make pie out of bitter apples and she did just that. Dora and Daniel, a married couple who were two of the oldest and longest employed migrants at the camp, answered their door to accept the delivery of a manila envelope. They opened it to find it contained a notice of a no-interest loan to start the flower nursery they had dreamed of. Hollering happily and waving the envelope, Dora rushed to share the news with her sewing-circle friends.

Carmen extended her vision of a self-sustaining community and UPS arrived one day and unloaded boxes of books. Besides poetry and novels, she had ordered dozens of books entitled *Get Green*—a textbook with lesson plans about how to turn a neighborhood economy into a flourishing green community replete with solar panels, barrels to catch and save rain, and organic gardening.

And as this was all happening, oil tankers packed with weed roared through the dead of night to docking stations in Las Cruces, were unloaded, and the marijuana was delivered to affluent neighborhoods in Santa Fe, Denver, Phoenix, Dallas, Santa Barbara, and Chicago, among other places.

30

September 2006

Casimiro thinks.

The light is on and I see him in the shed.

She gave that talk this afternoon, says a wound opens in her every time she enters the boss's house and sees his Mexican maids, gardeners, and cook. Opening the door and the yard gate and walking away from his yard, a wound opens in her.

She's a smart one that Carmen.

Wound of shame? Wound of rage? Wound over how they've treated Mexicans, Chicanos, Indios?

I, too, feel it in my muscles, my brain, my fingers and toes, the numbness on my right side. There's a red feeling like fire that pours from a crack inside me.

It is the wound-pain of not being recognized, entering a place and having no one greet you. Waiting at a table in a restaurant for a long time and no one comes to take your order. It is walking through a whole day and no matter where you go, there are citizens, media, organizations, and politicians telling you in every way that you don't matter, don't breathe, don't count, don't belong, don't deserve even floor crumbs of the American dream.

Carmen is right. For years he's been toying with us like we were one of his dogs, carrying on in his good-old-boy language of the rich.

He's hammered meaninglessness into me, burrowing a dark churning force of self-hate to the depths of my soul. I accepted it, part of the day, present in every breeze, in every row, in every leaf, every whack of the hoe, every bead of sweat trailing down my back, in every tractor and truck and sack. It anchored on a bone of despair and in my mind reproduced a thousand times, its ebb and flow consuming me until, reluctantly, I gave in to this fate of poverty, of no opportunity. Worthlessness.

The truth is we all have a choice to stay or leave and the fields didn't have cage bars on them. I could've left. But I didn't. And years later, after I vowed that my children would do better, would not have to endure the life I've had to, the light in the shed is on where Lorenzo is binding crates. Back a few years I should have stood with the protestors and boycotters and fought for a better life but I was afraid. I had my family and I sacrificed better paying jobs, accepted inhumane treatment, worked sixteen-hour days for three dollars an hour, but at least we had food on the table.

When I was eight, in Mexico, the American dream peered down on me from the stars, peeked at me from behind the moon, galloped through the canyons of my boyhood home and over the fields I loved and hated, nibbling the corn kernels that sprinkled the road from the cobs heaped on the tractor bumping up and down over tread ruts and wagon-wheel trenches. And like a happy dog out scaring birds from bushes, first light was a welcoming paradise to my eye.

I could smell the American dream in the sweet odor of cedar and juniper. At siesta time I was lulled by the peaceful notes a worker's accordion sounded from under the coolness of a wooden plank bridge, or I admired it in the religious statues carved from scrap wood and read its liturgical parables in the water irrigating our cornfield. I tell you, it was everywhere that was good.

When I killed that man in the hotel, it did something to my vision of the American dream. I prayed and prayed for forgiveness from God and tried to forget the crime I committed—maybe I didn't forget it, but I buried it. I felt it inside me but after a while I trained my mind not to visualize it.

I remember the first time the American dream took hold of me.

Its toddler's feet grew into my boots, its shoulders and arms stretched into my broadening shirt, it was enchanted using my brown eyes to see with. I was unable to contain my willingness to challenge myself to improve my life. I came without a passport, unknown. No birth certificate, green card, or anything else to label or pin me down.

Getting in those crops before they spoil still stands as the highest law of the land. Every cop; INS, DEA, or border patrol agent, judge or prosecutor knows that putting fruit, vegetables, and meat on the table comes first. If the slave work stopped, the American dream would stop— shrivel up and rot sure as an apricot on the ground. Food must be on the table. That is more important than the laws prohibiting Mexicans from entering America.

Imagine an America without wine, fish, bread, or catered banquets, without sweatshops to sew famous-name athletic gear, no Tiger Woods golf clubs, no Air Jordans, no Martha Stewart clothes, no clean streets.

That's why I am here, to service them, to make sure they pay low wages to make their money go further, to wash and change the oil on *their five trucks they never drive, to clean and keep up their three houses they never live in, to stand in line on fifteen-hour shifts in their chicken factories, pig farms, and slaughterhouses.*

If Americans don't get their way, the American dream breaks down, crumbles.

They'd challenge me to see who could cut or pick faster and I never lost: hippie, weed head, pool hustler, barber, mitote, wino, scavenger, charity case, beauty queen, whiner, and Mexican wannabe gringo—I beat them all.

I am close to the ground, with short legs and arms. I was fast.

Over the years, in the fields, I made many friends who returned to Mexico. And each Friday, at the end of the day, many of us workers walked down the dirt road to wait for the mailman, hoping for news from Mexico.

Away from home, we are a very lonely people, isolated from the world. We have no address, no number or name in the telephone book; no one outside of camp knows us. We raise our families prudently. In camp, we consider ourselves loving, religious, respectful people. Beyond camp, we are hunted down like criminals, considered aliens, and at any moment we can be handcuffed and hauled away like garbage in INS jeeps. Letters, then, keep many happy. I guess water understands dry soil the way I understand a letter from the few friends I've made.

But after forty years I am tired. Now, in my wheelchair, what use can they have for a worthless, worn-out old man?

The light still burns in the packing shed. My son works late.

Nopal would be proud of him. Her portrait has an unyielding claim on my heart. It hasn't been easy to carry on without her and I imagine what it would be like to have us together again.

On workdays I was always up before the roosters crowed or the trucks roared into the yard to load up workers; she'd be standing outside, slapping her gloves to ward off the chill. Sunday mornings we'd lie in bed and laugh and talk and eat. I'd wear my best and only suit for church, then afterward, friends would visit and she'd cook a big lunch. She would be made-up, her hair brushed out loosely, and in her red skirt and white blouse she looked stunning. Conjuring her face in my mind always sweeps away the warm ashes of remorse.

Her absence burns and, as always, the healing of the wound starts with looking at the land around me. Blue sky. Night stars. Moon. Sunlight on the leaves. And the magical air I breathed many a morning, I believe was drawn from the same place God lives.

I accept my stroke. I don't need to walk to enjoy the striking clarity of water streaming from the Rio Grande into ditches, or to inhale the fragrance of prairie plants—sumac, purple bee plant, ground lichen, juniper mistletoe. A good day draws me into the potential it possesses and the growing warmth of the morning makes me feel that something might happen to dispel the thorn of despair lodged in my throat—it digs deeper each day until it will scratch the surface of my heart and puncture it.

I stare up at the stars, distracted by guilt, thinking that I could have done something to prevent her death. I have become overly protective of Lorenzo. I didn't do a good job, though: Lorenzo is working late in the shed tonight. (If I look the other way, to the boss's house, I'll see they're playing tennis under the lights.) I should have given my sons a better life, at least a decent education. They deserve better. I hope they strike; I'll be with them, viva la huelga.

31

March 2007

Rafael finally agreed, after days of pleading and begging, to train Vito. Nine years ago he had made a solemn vow to La Virgen de Guadalupe that he would never enter into the boxing world again. He had managed his brother and he still blamed himself for his brother's death—from a blood clot in the brain while he was jogging on the ditch bank one morning. But seeing Vito box was like hearing God speak to his heart, telling him to guide Vito.

Before agreeing to train him, Rafael had to clear things with Puro. He laid down a set of rules that Puro had to swear he would abide by. Puro would put up all the money for training, food, travel, and equipment, and would set up the venues and do all the publicity. They knew what their roles were and they shook on it.

Rafael had witnessed such a phenomenon twice in his lifetime—Muhammad Ali and Roberto Durán—and he had never dared to imagine that one day he might manage and train a boxer of their caliber. But Vito was just as blessed and talented. Rafael watched the crowds and saw their reverence and awe for Vito, the beam of a growing star gleaming in their eyes, shining brighter than anyone imagined.

Rafa pulled in to the scrap yard and handed Vito an envelope of money. "You pulled it off, smart ass," he smiled, referring to last night's fight. "I thought he was going to kill you but you pulled it off. There's enough lettuce there to buy yourself some nice clothes."

Vito thumbed the bills the way a dealer shuffles cards and replied, "No faith. I could see it in your eyes."

Rafa shrugged.

"It's about the risk. That's what gets my heart going. And I'm just tuning up the carbs. Wait till you see me smoke the rubber. I need bigger fights."

A bunch of Vito's boxer friends were standing around nearby, including Ignacio, his coworker and corner man, who nodded in agreement.

"We could put an ad in the paper, take all comers. Headline it in the Sunday sports section."

"These are illegal," Rafa said. "You can't be advertising these fights."

"Yeah, but I got an idea. Come on, get out of the car and listen to it." With Rafa and Ignacio all ears, Vito started, "Rodeos. Me and my brother used to go to them all the time. Small towns have them. There's always these rich ranchers that show up, and when small towns gather, it's all about grudge matches—I mean hundred-year-old grudges, from way back to the conquistadores times. These small-village people have long memories of being slighted or treated unjustly. So and so stole family land, cheated cousin so and so, screwed the sister and left her. You get the drift? Everyone wants to settle an old score and they do it by betting."

"We set up a match there, and I'll tell you, some of those white ranchers got *bookoo* dollars. I want their money in my pocket: call it back wages. I'll collect for my parents, too. Hell, for all my peoples' back wages."

"I'll think about it. Rodeos?" Rafael said, shaking his head.

Inside his house, Rafael poured a cup of coffee from his thermos and sat down by the window. He had blamed himself for a long time when his brother died. He had been working him in the backyard, pushing him hard with the body bag, the speed bag, a little jump rope, sparring, and then a five-mile jog—when he fell—and he had died in Rafael's arms.

Rafael had told Vito one morning a week before, "When I saw you, that night I scuffled with Puro, in your first match, I didn't want to admit it but I saw it—those fists of yours, the natural flow of your feet, your head bobbing and shoulders weaving like you were dancing, clearly, you had magic. Understand one thing—God will be watching us."

Training started one morning when Rafa made Vito run up and back a mile along the riverbank of wet sand, carrying a knapsack of rocks. The monotony of the seamless sand made Vito fall into a trance, his lungs and legs numbed.

"It'll strengthen your ankles. *Hechale carbón!* Put yourself into it one more time. Thirty minutes, come on. Go, go, go."

A month later Rafael changed it up. "Now you train for agility," he said. "Roll, crouch, move left and right. Follow the path along the river and do not hit any branches in your way. Go to the Fourth Street bridge and turn back. Go!"

Rafael fine-tuned Vito's stance and the position of his hands and elbows, training him to duck, lean, and counterpunch. He ran him ten miles a day, had him sparring twenty rounds and slamming the body bag with such ferocity Rafa's shoulder stayed sore.

Vito slept deeply and, in the morning, still exhausted, he repeated the routine. He trimmed out jumping rope and pummeling the speed and midriff bag. One day blurred into the next, the only dividing line between night and day was pain, more pain.

He changed from being a backstreet scuffler into a sleek work of beauty. Precise punching made the ring the square sheet of white paper where he composed his poetry; his fancy footwork made observers stop what they were doing and look, his fists blocking or spring-loaded. His ferocity, under constant compression, could explode or prowl for the right time to strike or counter.

Every day at noon, Vito sat on a picnic bench outside the gym, drinking a strawberry soda, eating tamales and burritos from a chuck wagon in the parking lot. Lowrider kids leisurely reclined on car fenders; they liked hanging around him. Boxers from other gyms came to see him work out and their presence re-charged and powered him—he wanted them to take the message: he was the best.

Legend grew around him. Word got around that he'd made his shoes from a deer he'd caught on foot, and gossip branched into myth, becoming a story of how he'd taken it down with his own bare hands.

Leaning his arms and shoulders on the ropes every day at workouts, Rafa would yell, "Remember the lesson: let no man take your corner. It's yours, all you have, you die defending that corner. Theirs is on the street, yours is in the ring. But nobody, nobody, comes to take your corner—you understand?

"Never forget those kids on the streets—addicted, homeless, in gangs and without hope, in despair—but still, how they're willing to die to defend a concrete curb, willing to fight protecting their corner on a dingy street without lights and worth nothing. Nothing in the universe is theirs except a little corner on a dark street smelling of vomit and drunk's piss and littered with junkie needles and crack pipes and vials. A corner, it's all they have of heaven, but it means everything to them, makes them visible to the world that makes them invisible, makes them count in a world that discounts them, and they're prepared to kill for that corner, to give up their lives for that small dark piece of hell.

"Now you show me how you'll protect your corner. Last man standing, let's see it, let's see it!"

32

I am the afternoon sand that the gust scatters. Inhaled into lungs and nostrils and swallowed by mouths, I fuse into bloodstreams, blend into beating hearts, and swell into pulses. So strange that I learn new things about my family, am inhaled into the lungs of my son Vito, always the defender of the poor, balancing justice scales in the ring when the courts always favor the rich. Words reverberate in his marrow and beneath his tongue and in the back of his brain with a mysterious vibration that hums in his soul, rippling into ever-deepening unknown in himself. The strange power he feels when he speaks to the crowd lingers in his mouth long after a fight.

I am his breath when he steps to his corner, flinging his head back to loosen up his neck muscles. He disrobes, bounces on the balls of his feet, and, as the announcer calls out his name and points to his corner and Vito raises his hand, his corner is the center of the universe.

It isn't like he wants to be a leader. In fact, the first time he heard himself say anything provocative was more to get people to pay to see him fight than to be a human-rights activist.

His talent as a boxer neutralizes the powers of cops, judges, and border patrol agents—defies their authority. Each punch relays the message that he waited all his life for this and he vaguely understood its power. The words he uses to give them pride pushes out from inside him. He has no credentials, no diploma, nothing to point out that his experience is theirs.

But he knows that behind his verbal provocations and his clownish antics, he makes people turn their attention to him, he intrudes on their space until they acknowledge him.

As the words come forth from his heart, strung together like grains of rice, to people holding out their souls like wooden bowls, his words feed some deep hunger in their hearts. He would yell out to them, making them count, bringing a smile to their malnourished hearts.

And, if only temporarily in time and space, he was one of them and his champion presence made up for their lack of money. His taking a beating round after round made sense of their tortuous crossing of dangerous deserts on foot. His facing fighters intent on destroying him made sense of evading the armed gangs of smugglers and traffickers who wanted to rob, rape, and kidnap them. He gave their survival dignity not disgrace.

When Vito was knocked down, then on one knee, catching his breath, when they saw him rise to go on, it wove into their memories of fording flood-raging rivers and almost being drowned before catching a second wind and moving on to the other side.

Boxing fans believed he had at one time gone without food or shelter, been detained and worked back-breaking labor, and that he was, daily, punished in countless ways for being Chicano in a society ruled by the rich. And when Vito cried out to them, the crowd went wild with joy. He posed the question: Make it a crime to serve hot meals to illegal immigrants? I say feed them! Prosecute, imprison, deport you? No, my brothers, I don't think so! You deserve admiration! Welcome! Welcome to America!

33

July 2007

Pickups creaking with people eased up to the mountains east of Albuquerque and headed north from the Mexican-owned cement plant nestled in the hills to the Sandia Peak picnic grounds.

It was César Chávez day and Mexicans and Chicanos had spent the hot morning marching in the streets for justice and equal rights, so many people that they shut the city down for hours. With the march over, a sense of renewal permeated the air and peoples' complexions seemed to glow with hope. Barbecues flavored the air and the parks were filled with grandparents, toddlers, lovers, and pick-up football games. As music blared Los Lonely Boys and Los Lobos, lowrider kids walked among the people, hawking tickets for the night's fight between Vito and the favorite, ranked ninth, named Phoenix, who was the draw for now. Vito was determined not to waste time with him, he would go in and pluck and fry him in the fire flames of his jabs and uppercuts, beat him down.

Later that afternoon, Vito met Rafa in the worker's locker room at the cement plant. Vito suited up, laced his beautiful blue and red beaded deerskin shoes, sparred and danced around to break a sweat. He talked to himself to work up a fighting fever, visualized himself left, right, counterpunching, and upper hooking the opponent down.

Crowds started showing up and fans of all nationalities and colors poured into the huge warehouse used for storing and shipping cement bags. The giant loading-dock doors swung open and more people streamed in, queuing up in the betting line that snaked its way to where bookies were taking all comers. Puro was among them and, flanked by bodyguards, he put his money on the table. He waved to Vito and gave Rafael a nod that meant, "take care of business."

The announcer entered the ring and took the mic but before he could even start to say a word Vito grabbed it. Everyone was shocked. Rafa didn't know what to do. He looked at Puro to see if this was some kind of behind-closed-doors betrayal and he could tell by Puro's puzzled expression that he was equally confused. Not even Ignacio, who was standing in the ring in the corner, knew what to expect. He shrugged and shook his head at Rafa.

Vito roared into the mic, "This is a worker's fight and the ring is a people's court where I am judge and jury. People are marching out there for basic rights." He paused. "This afternoon, *caballeros y trabajadores,* migrants workers and Chicanos, you were supposed to see preliminary matches by two boxers from Tijuana but they didn't make it. No," he yelled with an indignant pitch. "Why? *La pinche migra* got them, wouldn't let them pass the border. *La pinche migra* is going to pay today for that. Why? Because do you know what kind of work Phoenix does when he's not training? He works for ICE, the worst kind of *la migra!*" The drama soared and the crowd reeled with hysterical satisfaction that their suffering now had a target.

Vito gave the mic back to the ref, who looked at Phoenix for proof of Vito's allegation but even Phoenix seemed bewildered, moving his head sideways, in shock, trying to convey that it wasn't true, but the crowd took it as defying Vito's threat to beat him up.

Then, before the ref could start the fight, Vito swiped the mic out of his hand again and blurted out, "Build a wall on the border? I'll beat it down and crush it with these!" He waved his gloves. "Make an honest working immigrant a felon? Fuck you, Congress, fuck you, senators! I offer amnesty to all of you living and working here!"

They clapped, whistled, and cried out, rocking the dock and warehouse roof. They came from everywhere: techies, military men in helicopter jackets, tow-truck drivers, bikers with Nazi helmets, gangbangers, gamblers on their way down, drug dealers on their way up, security guards, bus drivers, Indios and tattooed Mohawk gringos, secretaries, nose-studded runaways, goth speed freaks, skateboarders, and more. The room was thick with Old Spice, cigar smoke, and the smell of fried chorizo and tacos.

Vito put his index finger to his lips to quiet the spectators, and then he added, "I want Phoenix to stand down, just for a little bit. Not to disappoint, since there'll be no runner-up fights to the main show, but I need to warm up and I'll bet my purse tonight that I can take anybody in this warehouse. One round a person. Puro collects the money. So, anybody wants a piece of me, you cops and narcs and detectives in the crowd, come get your piece of kick ass now."

Two tattooed Italians shouldered through the crowd to put their money down. Vito went to his corner and Ignacio, waiting there, whispered, "What the fuck's up?"

"Making money."

"You don't know shit. These Mexicans know how to fight, you don't know what you're getting into." His eyes were on two Mexicans who were hurrying outside. Through the warehouse doors, Ignacio watched them huddle with a group of men gathered in a corner. They all put their money together and the Mexicans dashed back inside.

One of the Mexicans placed the pile of bills in front of Puro on the table, and though Puro wanted to tell the Mexican he wasn't taking any bets on Vito's offer, he knew a riot would ensue if he refused, so he counted the money and wrote down the amount on the wager sheet. It was Vito's most hotheaded move yet and it pissed him off so much he couldn't speak. Others lined up and he begrudgingly took the cash and wrote down their bets.

Puro saw two Mexican men moving through the crowd and recognized one of them: he had retired years earlier, but was a seasoned fighter from Juárez, ranked in his prime, who knew he could, with a little luck, destroy Vito.

Puro's concern magnified a hundred times when he saw a massive bull-shouldered Mexican enter through the corrugated iron sliding doors and a gasp escaped from the crowd. A pair of green-red-white Mexican-colored gloves were slung over one shoulder. The migrants recognized him as one of the pickers and as he passed everyone patted his shoulders. There was a commotion, everyone talking at once, and Puro realized that he couldn't stop the matches now. If he tried, they'd take his actions for reneging and he'd end up getting stabbed, or worse.

He left the table and walked over to Vito, who was waving an eagle feather over himself and fanning smoke from a piece of cedar that was burning in a rock bowl.

"You think that fucking feather dumb-fuck Ignacio gave you is going to help your ass against *that*? Do you have any clue who the fuck he is? You stupid son of a bitch, what the fuck have you fucking done? You lose, I'll kill you. No one fucks with me like this. No one!"

But instead of being repentant, Vito replied calmly, "After this, you're in for an ass whopping like you've never had in your life." He then mimicked Puro, "What the fuck have you done?"

Vito scanned the faces of the mob—they were unruly, excited, boisterous. He could not have been happier and he closed his eyes, praying and waving the feather over his chest and arms.

Vito placed the feather back into the paper bag and smiled at Rafa, who was staring at him an inch from his face. He told Rafa, "I don't mean disrespect, *tío,* but this Chicano, I am not a fucking joke. This Chicano is here to collect his dues. It's not funny—now you can let my arm go."

"After tonight, I won't be able to get you a match anywhere. You'll be a laughingstock."

"I'm not going to shame you or myself." Vito stared off, his eyes floating above the crowd, then he continued. "Those jokes about Chicanos betraying the mother country, that we're not as tough as Mexicans, well, tonight I'm putting those ideas to sleep and rewriting history. They ain't seen the power of Vito's voodoo." He raised his arms as supporters cried out in favor. "These two hot peppers, grown in the fields of oppression and poverty, are going to bring tears tonight."

He sidestepped, danced left and right, did a few switchback moves, and then Rafa tapped his shoulder, "Okay, Elvis, let's get it."

Vito stared across the ring to his first opponent, one of the Italians, Mario, whose eyes were hard with wrath.

"Every minute you stare at me like that, I'm gonna take out a tooth. Mexican dentistry, Chicano style," Vito said.

The crowd was whipped into a frenzy.

Ignacio pulled out his pearl-handled knife from his sock and slipped it into his pocket. "You're talking so much shit we're going to need this."

A different ref, a short Mexican still wearing his brick-laying clothes, gray concrete dust on his boots, pants, and gray palms, stepped between the boxers and waved them in.

"Okay, you know the rules—last man standing. Have a good clean fight." Although the tone of his instructions was impartial, his eyes glazed with contempt when he glanced at Vito.

The fighters circled a few minutes until Mario flexed the rattlesnakes of his huge arms and uncoiled two fists, striking a left that slammed Vito in the chest and lifted him off the floor. Vito winced, rubbed at the burning in his chest, then immediately he was bobbing and weaving, counterpunching, protecting the sore place on the left side of his chest. He pretended he was tired and covered up as he drew the big man in but then he responded furiously, attacking with a blinding flurry of powerful jabs. Vito dazed the giant and then launched an overhand and caught his jaw. Even spectators six and seven people back heard something shatter. The concrete shuddered with two hundred and twenty pounds of dead weight colliding against it.

Vito gave a toothy grin as he danced around the ring. He saw the alarm in Ignacio's expression just as the second Italian fighter hit him from behind and Vito stumbled forward.

A little wobbly, he turned and said, "Oh, you want to play. Well, let's play my way. *Andale cabrón,* let's fry up some meatballs and boil the spaghetti."

Vito knocked him out in eleven seconds.

Next was a tall bone-gaunt biker. He spit tobacco and motioned Vito to bring it on.

"Let's get the steak on the grill," Vito said. He entertained the crowd, asking, "How you want it, medium-well, well-done? With a little blood?"

Blood was the resounding answer. A bunch of white bikers sporting clubhouse bandannas and sleeveless denim jackets with gang patches growled for Vito's dismemberment. And as Vito was squaring up for the barbecue, another biker, built more across than up and down, stepped into the fray. Whatever rules they might have abided by evaporated and to up the ante, a third biker—adorned with facial tattoos and with a red swastika cut across his washboard stomach muscles—frowned, slapped his low brow, smacked his jaw and flat nose, and snarled, "I want my money, bitch."

They bum-rushed him and the audience roared but, undeterred, Vito crouched low, protecting his head, and provoked them even as a hail of fists and elbows came at him from all sides. After they tired of beating him and were gasping, arms dangling at their sides, Vito did a quick one-two move with his feet and spurted away from the corner, telling them, "Let's see what we got here now." He slapped his gloves together, flared his nostrils, and, snorting in short bursts, he moved in.

Blood and snot ran, their heads swelled up like soccer balls and their eyelids puffed shut. He was easily fending off their sluggish attempts at hitting him and countering with a marksman's precision. Blow after blow opened new cuts. The crowd was rabid for knockouts, but Vito was punishing the fighters, working each section of their body until it cracked, bled, purpled, and oozed.

He focused his uppercuts, midsection crunches, right crosses to the face, snappy jabs, and powerhouse lefts. Their faces resembled nothing, each a mass of welts and gashes, bleeding skin rags.

The spectators grew concerned and disbelief widened their eyes but Vito would not relent. He hit harder, spraying blood into the crowd. And his three opponents rallied only to be crushed, charged only to be rebuffed, until finally they fell and had to be dragged off.

Vito, as usual, pranced on his tiptoes, a thoroughbred still anxious to run. And then, from his blind side, another man flung himself at Vito, attempting to lock him in a bear hug and hold him, but Vito butted him with an elbow and landed a right to the ear and the would-be warrior crumpled. And Vito kept beating him, even though he was on his knees, inhaling and drinking his own blood. Vito then knelt down beside the man and, from a kneeling position, punched at him until the crowd filled the place with a deafening demand for Phoenix.

Here and there certain fans were getting unruly. Friends of the beat-up fighters pushed their way through the standing-room-only crowd as people tried to stop them. In the commotion, Puro's thugs closed ranks around Vito, each cradling a handgun that they'd clearly have no qualms about using.

Vito yelled out to Puro, "A joke, eh? Nobody's laughing now."

The Phoenix fight was the last match of the night and by then Vito had psyched him out so badly that after a few punches Phoenix went down. After that night, and for the next seven months, Vito climbed the ranks to become a serious contender. But that didn't keep him from fighting off the record, and the people adored him.

34

October 2007

While he waited for Carmen to arrive at the warehouse, Lorenzo decided to pack some chili. The conveyor belt looped in and out at the blemish stations, then the spray station, then carried the chili to the end where workers alongside the belt plucked and packed. It was at this time of the evening—seven—that his mother used to bring him to the warehouse to pack, and the resinous fragrance of the chili brought back memories that made him forget Carmen was late.

He missed his mother and recalled that she used to say how nice and soft the tortilla dough felt in her palms, drawing out the aches from her fingers and forearms. He'd seen the scarred claws of other workers, the blistered husks or whatever you want to call what passed as human hands. Every part of the body bore the mark of excessive work, even dreams—he'd often hear his father mutter in his sleep, whimpering from pain, hurrying from the rows to the sheds, his knees swollen with arthritis. Now he just grunted. His mother, however, used to tell him she came up with songs while rolling and kneading dough; the constant rhythm of rolling and squeezing gave her lyrics a soft roll. "Tortilla dreams" she called those songs.

There was another part of his mother few knew about.

When she got up and dressed before the sun rose, when the trucks came into the camp to load up the workers, he noted how she listened to their voices with sorrow. When he looked at her sitting in the back of the truck he saw she loathed the chili fields and he saw, after each day, how she vigorously scrubbed at the dirt and the day's dried sweat that coated her body.

There was no such thing as a promotion or a high position in the camp. You might have a different title, but everyone had to work in the fields. His mother sometimes stared with envy and resentment at the motorists pulling up to the stands at the end of the dirt road. Women from Las Cruces and El Paso, wearing flowing Spanish pleated-hem skirts, white blouses, and sunglasses, sat in their cars while the workers loaded their trunks with melons, chili, and squash.

He knew the woman part of her, sensed her female desire in the way she sprinkled water into the flour on the cutting board. He saw how while the neighbors chatted in the kitchen she would drift into a reverie while flattening the dough smooth, flipping it back and forth between her hands and placing it on the *comal*.

Standing at the front door, behind the screen, facing the compound and fields, she imagined leaving the camp with Casimiro and going to Chicago, where her singing career could flourish. Lorenzo could tell she'd been trapped—Casimiro loved her and she could not leave him—yet when she scanned the labor camp a deep loathing suffocated her. She had seen too much of it, smelled too much, and she had to fight off the terrible thoughts that crept into her heart—thoughts of packing up and leaving, especially when those cowboys came in with trailers to pick up hay. They looked at her in such a way that their eyes followed her into her bed.

Once a month on the weekend, she joined the other camp women going into town for groceries. Walking the aisles she studied the white women: strangers with unhappy faces, dyed and styled haircuts, they were fat and thin, pale creatures in workout clothes, their lives seemingly as neat as stainless steel forks and spoons lined up in a silverware drawer.

She was invisible to them. She learned a long time ago to avoid eyes, to never complain, to conduct herself in public as a prisoner of war.

After shopping, the white women would go back to their private, secure worlds and she would return to the flat iron plate on the woodstove, to sprinkling the exact amount of flour on the cutting board, powdering another dough ball, and kneading it out round. Fear coiled at the pit of her stomach, fear for her future, of growing prematurely old; fear worked into her eyes, fingertips, ears, and legs, rattling a warning of wariness at vehicles in the distance raising a cloud of dust coming down the road.

She'd wrap the stack of tortillas in a towel to keep them warm and then, hiding behind them, she'd make her way to the baptism, wedding, funeral, party, or communal meeting, and when Monday came, she'd give the grower her labor, her pride, her sweat, until nothing was left.

But never respect.

Carmen was so much like her.

35

Carmen entered the packing shed, set her backpack down, and crept up to hug Lorenzo. The migrant meeting had gotten her worked up. Talking about rights, strikes for higher wages, and a healthier work environment made her adrenaline pump faster, ignited her libido.

She resisted the compulsion to slam Lorenzo down on his back, yank his pants off, and straddle him on the sawdust, kicking crates aside. She wanted to get that hot stinging red chili juice on her lips and suck him until he cried out in pain and ran butt-ass naked to the water trough outside to soak his dick in cold water. Teach him to sulk.

She asked, "You mad at me?" The question made him irritable. She hated when he was moody, so preoccupied that all he could manage was a morose smile. She thought, *the hell with him,* and started for the door.

He clicked the conveyor belt switch off.

She stopped.

"Okay," he started, "but now that we have a little money coming in we can't afford a boycott, a march on the newspapers and TV stations, or to petition the governor to investigate. No more meetings for a while."

She reached into her backpack and pulled out a book. She

placed the book down on the table under a lamp next to the conveyor belt. "Read this. Read it aloud, this paragraph."

He skimmed the highlighted phrases. "The proportion of those who will labor under all hardships of life, and secretly sigh for a more equal distribution of its blessings . . . Freedom without opportunity . . . manipulation of their attitudes and behavior . . . and the best gift we can offer the suffering masses is to free them from the delusion that they have a right to live."

He hesitated.

He had always been afraid of words, scared of their hidden meanings. When she first met him, she noticed that every legal letter he got in the mail he tossed in the trash and when she asked him why, he said he didn't want to know what was inside. Poison hidden in words.

"You're stirring up trouble and I don't want him kicking you out like he did my brother." She followed him to a semicircle of torn armchairs in front of an old black-and-white television against the wall, where workers watched soaps and sports. "Things are going good. The kids enjoy the soccer field, women are into their quilting circles, and the doctor is making daily visits. I don't want to mess stuff up."

"It's true," she insisted. "You've done a lot, but you don't change people's lives, I mean permanently, with sports. Change the way they think about what they can do in the world and everything is possible and every one of them will be a champion in their own eyes."

"That's the last thing we need. We can go on like we are: money improves our lives. Money's the key."

Carmen tried choosing the right words but said it the way she knew best, straight and direct. "I can't do that."

He looked at her.

She replied, looking directly into his eyes, "I love you like no other man I've ever come close to loving, and I want to marry you, but we have a chance now to do something and we should do it. Please."

"You came here to do your studies, why don't you just do that, focus on finishing it? You're taking this poor-people thing too serious. Turning your studies into a mission to lead people out of their hardships? No, it's not what this is about."

"Read," she tapped the page with her index finger.

"Your being a savior might end me up in jail. If the cops or DEA came around, I'd be in deep shit."

"Lorenzo, I am so tired of you having to look in your rear-view mirror all the time. Your cell phone ringing day and night. You're out late, you can barely get out of bed in the morning, and your business associates from El Paso and Las Cruces are always high."

He stood up. "Didn't you hear what I just said?"

"But that's not what we're doing. Our group will open doors in people's hearts." If only she could convey what she was feeling without sounding too lofty. Explain how the sky, wind, soil, and water give the field-workers purpose. Explain how these elements live beside them in an intimate existence, how the elements were extensions of their bodies, shaping their hands, and molding their legs to their demands.

She continued, "We're not going to march or protest, just file grievances and present them to Mr. Miller. And you know what, love means leaving the heart wild, so don't try and tame mine."

He gazed at her for a long minute and then shook his head, realizing that there was no way to convince her to stop organizing. He continued reading the phrases highlighted in yellow. "And people have no rights beyond what they can obtain . . . astounding success of propaganda . . . ignorance and stupidity of the masses, controlled for their own good . . . the ignorant and vulgar are as unfit to judge the modes of government as they are unable to manage its reins . . . slaughtering the natives, English style, so that the misguided creatures . . . its public relations . . . turn working people into objects . . . as stupid and ignorant as it is possible for a human creature to be . . . when in favor of the masters . . . the government or owners of industry are their only possible savior."

He slapped the book shut. "This shit's crap."

"They're shoving it up our ass every day."

He flicked the ON switch to the conveyor belt, drowning her voice out.

She flipped the switch off.

"Knock it off, Carmen."

"*You* cut the shit," she demanded.

Rain started beating hard on the zinc roof, the moisture making the air smell like a bait shop.

He looked up at the rafters and said, "We need the rain."

She answered, "Thank god, it's about time."

They sat on the chairs and listened, watched lightning *whoosh* through the air like a giant machete cutting across the green fields. Lights flickered and the electricity went out.

She's right, he thought. He was stepping up the ranks financially, he was still a gutsy field-worker, but maybe he was losing his scrub-brush approach to life. It used to be he didn't need much to survive and didn't ask for much. Along the way something had happened to change that.

Her voice came out of the dark. "I love you."

She groped and reached, their fingers touched, and they tumbled into a crib of just-picked corncobs. In the soft crackle of leaves and thunder, he whispered, "I love you, too, and I'm sorry I hurt you."

His belt buckle flashed and her blouse buttons were ripped off.

Her hair smelled like clear blue sky along the river, her breath like cottonwood leaves blowing out the warehouse doors, brimming ankle high on the ground, bunched up at fence lines. And then there was a hush as she groaned, then silence followed as she shivered, a reverent quiet shiver as if monks were chanting music from within her, stirring in his soul a sense of ancient belonging.

Bright lights flashed in his head. He was in the chute, he tightened the leather strap around the mare's stomach, pulled the slack until it was snugly wrapped around his hand.

She banged against the chute sides and the gate flung open. She zigzagged and whip-snapped and he felt himself airborne. One moment he could smell her skin and taste her sweat, and the next moment everything went blank. He came to in the warehouse, on the couch, with Carmen at his side.

"What the hell happened?" He raised himself on one elbow.

"When it comes to loving an amazing woman, you were pissing in a hurricane," she smiled. "You hungry?" She offered him a corncob. "It stopped raining. I'm going for walk," she said.

"I'm going with you." He struggled to get up.

He washed his crotch at the water trough by the corral. The air smelled of livestock and she followed the music of water down a ravine where a creek ran.

Carmen watched the water. "It's time, honey," she said to Lorenzo and sat beside him.

"Time?"

"To get out of the business. I don't want to live wary of every stranger, guarded, afraid it might be the last day together before they haul you off to jail."

"Just now, in the warehouse, it was like you lifted me in this two-hundred-mile-an-hour wind. Are you okay? I didn't hurt you, did I?"

She stared at the water. She was sad and didn't know why. But she spoke anyway, "When I came, butterflies fanned out across my mind, millions of butterflies released from my thighs, migrating out from the center of my soul, covering the sun, the moon." She started crying and said, "Hold me, Lorenzo, I'm scared."

He held her in silence, their breathing bringing them together, knees drawn up, arms and hands clutched tight.

"You feeling better?" he asked.

"Look," she pointed at two mallards floating serenely amid the weeping willow branches drooping into the water.

"That's the way you get married," she said. "You just know you belong together, that you were born for each other."

Lorenzo knew she meant the two of them, and said, "Yep."

She thought, not so much in words but in feelings, *Take away my body, my books, my mind, and you have left an anger forged on the anvil of my heart. But take away my man and I am alone. Feel alone. Every time I talk up, go into a store, walk down the street, I'm alone.*

My anger goes deep and it would be bottomless if I ever lost you, Lorenzo. How I love you and how you seem to be falling down a long dark hole. I hear a train-crossing bell in my heart, warning you the train is coming, but you try to beat the train and it's faster than you, baby, faster than you.

36

Interpretations are as abundant as chili leaves—and mine are as wrong or right as any person's. Because I birthed my boys doesn't mean I understand them. Raising a family and singing at night was real enough but my sons had a magic that lifted my spirit beyond all earthly pleasures.

Lorenzo does not sacrifice a good man to the uncivilized rabble. He tells them no, you may not make martyrs of the innocent. And when he speaks, the arrangements of words are patterned on the teachings of earthquakes.

There is a way to satisfy your vision without having to co-opt it. There is a way to see the deeper reality where spirits reside, as with the guitar, but the strings have snapped, Lorenzo, and you must learn the sorrow of the captive, learn the hard way that silence and jail bars are not an option for us.

37

May 2008

Instead of marching on the international bridge between Juárez and El Paso, in the May 1 solidarity march with Carmen and the immigrant women, Lorenzo lay on his back with his forearm over his face, pressing down on his eyes. He had gone with friends to El Paso to a few bars, then to someone's house to talk business and do a few lines. The cops came and found an eight ball of cocaine on the table and everyone in the house was taken into custody and charged with possession.

Every hour or so the police brought in protestors by the dozens, reminding Lorenzo that he should have been out there with them. They talked about how they'd crossed police lines and he could sense the pride in their voices.

The talk in the cell was loud.

A white guy was saying, "Occupy a country we have no business in?"

A young Mexican replied, dreaming of the future day when he'd return in uniform, citizenship papers in hand, "I'm ready to go whenever."

"You don't think there's something wrong with that," an

older woman asked, "that the government offers citizenship to any Mexican who signs up to fight in Iraq?"

There was almost a fight when some guy by the bars, looking out on the tier, shouted out, "It's your manhood—not to sign up means you a bitch."

"Fuck you," a Mexican said from the other end of the cell. His female companion grabbed his wrist and held him.

A white kid wearing a UTEP T-shirt joined in. "It's bullshit. Politicians fill their pockets, every one of them are corrupt muthafuckers."

"I'll tell you what," an elderly Indian woman with graying hair said, "if the only way of proving you're a worthy American is to grab a gun and engage in a war, then why don't they send their own daughters and sons?" And, after a pause, she added, "My son Daniel was killed over there."

A guard swung the tank gate open and a trusty handed out baloney sandwiches and cartons of milk.

Everybody ate in silence.

A middle-aged man with a bad limp got up from his cot, went to the bars, and threw his milk carton out on the tier. He turned around to the prisoners. "What happens, if you're patriotic and *do* go to war, is that when you come back, people look at you with hate like you're a monster." He glared. There was something about his disposition that made any counterresponse dangerous.

"I used to believe," he went on, his voice melting to a softer tone, "that an education meant starting a new life. Meant that with hard work an education could get you to places you never imagined. The degree, the paper with your name, could not be taken back, it proved you had earned it."

Silence.

"But nothing! I got nothing but sweeping up the garbage, cleaning rooms, carrying out trash. Smart ass, when that happens, then what?"

The air vibrated in every ear, silence swung back and forth like a live utility wire snapped in a storm. Everybody knew he was talking about himself.

Lorenzo felt what the man was saying. He, too, felt there was a hole in his soul, felt how he held up his one stick of hope and burned it like a torch, trying to find his way out of the sewer tunnel of his life.

Self-loathing whittled him down to nothing.

He got up, looked out the window. A couple of miles beyond, ducks, geese, and cranes descended on fields under an inch of irrigation water, the water's sunset reflection lulling him into a serene hypnosis. The fields had a calming effect, though he knew the bucolic scene masked the misery the pickers endured.

When he was three or four, they'd eat blue cornmeal for breakfast before boarding the truck. The brothers slept in the same bed, face to feet. Casimiro stuffed kindling into the small cast-iron box lined with bricks and Lorenzo would watch the flames shoot up through the small cracks in the siding. They waited inside the Pullman until one of them whispered, "Here comes the truck!" Then, in the darkness, engine sputtering steam, muffler grumbling low and spitting black exhaust at the ground where spasmodic coughs puffed up dirt as if the weight of more field-workers climbing in was too much for it to bear, they climbed in the back.

Some of the seasonal migrants worked for just a week or a few days. They were social dropouts, aging rejects, and grim-lipped cadavers, opening eyes to a morning sun suspended like a corpse on a tree, bones bleached, pecked by buzzards.

Even their boots were patched, their shirts and trousers stunk of landfills, and the small handful of their soul seemed to visibly rise to the surface of their skin like scabs medicated with leaf juice, bandaged in dirt. They were the road-cracked ones, dispossessed, who couldn't find a place in life, bulging eyes, thin arms, muttering at the air.

He could hardly look at them. A furtive shame branded their features, marked their gestures and talk, blemished their demeanor. Dark-skinned whites and Mexicans bedded down with bad luck at day's end and it frightened him that such a morose role in life lay in wait for him. He prayed that God would protect him from such a frightening fate.

A part of him yearned to invite them home to wash their piss-stained pants, tweeze splinters from their palms, blow his breath on them as if they were dying embers, his child's tenderness reddening their grief to something that glowed in the dark. But even at five he was aware how despair could not be washed off. The anguish had drilled itself down deep until nothing but the dust of their despair remained, debris of shattered wholeness, intact enough to allow them to bend and pick and carry bags to the truck, but that was all.

He remembered even earlier, when his mom would bundle him in blankets, at four or four thirty in the morning, still dark, and carry them over to Mrs. Quintana's house, the camp grandma, where other working parents brought their kids and they'd be there all day, crawling around on the dirt floor smoothed by dozens of crawling baby knees and hands to a shiny brown tile.

When he started picking up bad habits from other kids, Nopal kept them with her. Strapping Vito to her breast with a sling, holding Lorenzo in her arm, she climbed into the truck with workers asleep in the back, packed shoulder to shoulder, ready with gloves, the women in their cardboard bonnets secured with safety pins, cloth covering the sides.

With his forearm over his eyes he remembered how he and his mama picked together. She'd pull out her sack, which she had sewn herself, embroidered with the names of her children and husband, with roses and hearts and hummingbirds, and she'd sing, moving through the rows.

If you got sick, with diarrhea, headache, or a snake or spider bite, you curled up in the shade of the water truck, next to the tire, and slept your illness off. The hours were broken by talk, lifting your head at the distant horizon—dreaming of a driver's contract with farmers, begging the landowner to give his field to them, that was the big prize—but you had to speak English, be respected by the workers.

When Miller leased Casimiro a field, he was elevated to *el majordomo,* and was responsible for the hiring and firing of workers, keeping the trucks moving from field to warehouse, making sure shipments were dispatched in a timely manner.

He remembered lunch break, left his picking sack, and found a shady spot by the truck. There were no trees, only the hot dirt that burned right through boots. He exchanged a jalapeño for an apple, a piece of cheese for a tortilla, rice for beans, taco for burrito. And after lunch, he went to the rows again, and he saw himself bending down and snapping the chili off when a guard called his name and he was escorted from his cell to the visitor's room.

38

August 2008

It had been almost four years since they had seen each other and even though Vito had not called ahead of time, he had no problem getting into the El Paso county jail. His unexpected arrival stirred the otherwise morose atmosphere with excitement. The jailers greeted him with pads and pens for autographs, the convicts crowded the front of the cage that opened on the common area to catch a glimpse of Vito.

In the visiting room, Vito turned his nose up, sniffed, and sneezed. He looked around.

Carmen explained "It's the mace and pepper spray the cops used on the marchers. I just barely made it out of there before the police swarmed in."

Lorenzo entered and the brothers hugged and squeezed each other's arms.

"What the hell for?" Vito asked Carmen.

"Immigrants," Carmen said, "were marching for civil rights." She beamed.

Lorenzo asked, "Did you go to the camp? See how much we did? Does Miller know you were there?"

Vito gave him another big hug. "It looks great and I didn't ask permission."

"Man, it is *so* nice to see you, *carnal*." Lorenzo was genuinely glad. "Sorry it had to be like this."

"How's everyone doing, my old partners still out there— Ramiro, Armando, Omar?"

"They're around, keeping tabs on your career. But a lot of them moved away."

"The workers living in the trailers by the river were wiped out by the flood," Carmen said. "Their trailers floated down the interstate and within hours those nasty developers came in, wrote out checks for their lots, and rumor has it that by next year we'll have gated communities next to camp—mansions on the river. Believe that shit?"

Lorenzo mused, "Yeah, the rains were bad, but everything else seems to be coming down on our heads. Come on, sit down, sit down."

They sat at a small steel table reserved for inmates and visitors. In the guard's cubicle, guards from other parts of the jail kept streaming in to see if it was true, was Vito really in the jail?

Vito recalled, "We used to sit on the ditch bank fishing, talked a million times about somehow making it out of the fields. Well, we're here. You ready now, *carnal*?" Vito clenched his fist, pumped it up and down, turned his head toward heaven, and said, "Teaming up!"

"I'll manage you, we'll get a title shot."

"When do you get out?"

Carmen interjected, "Talk business later." She stood and pushed between them, showering Lorenzo with kisses.

Lorenzo muttered as he was being smothered. "I'm a first-time offender. No sweat. I got a hearing and they'll set my bail and in four days . . ."

Lorenzo and Carmen sat holding hands. "I want you to take Carmen to San Diego, load up whatever she has there, and by the time you come back, I'll be out."

She was puzzled.

"Take tomorrow off. I'll see you when you come back. We're moving our marriage date up." He smiled at her.

"Serious?" Vito asked.

"Oh God," Carmen steadied herself.

"Dude, that ain't no way to do it. Get on your knees *vato!*" Vito chided Lorenzo.

"I already did, some months ago, but I'll do it again." He knelt and proposed to her a second time. He wiped her tears away with his tongue and held her. The guards, the cons, and the visitors clapped.

Regaining her composure she asked, "And the business?"

He combed her hair with his fingers. "It's over, done with. We have enough saved up."

"Congratulations," Vito offered. "I'm so damn happy you're finally going to get your act together."

Lorenzo rocked her back and forth in his arms while over her shoulder he said to Vito, "And you better get ready, I'm working you out twice a day, five times a week. A title shot would give us the money we need."

"For?" Carmen asked.

"Miller's land. I've got quite a bit saved up, but I want to buy a whole section, six hundred acres. He said if we came up with the cash, he'd sell it to us. And you, little brother," he pointed with his index finger, "and I are going to own that land, build our homes, and start our own farm."

39

After the visit, Vito and Carmen returned to the camp. They exited I-25 and drove west for two miles and turned right at the long dirt road where the fruit stands were. Vito was surprised to see no trucks, cars, or vans parked bumper to bumper beside the fields and no workers. The endless stretch of chili fields looked empty. He passed Miller's place and was stopped by a mob of migrants gathered on the road. A helicopter flew above them.

"What's going on?" Vito asked.

Carmen pointed to the river, and through the trees Vito saw police escorting migrants in handcuffs to three ICE vans. "What the fuck's that?"

"They were protesting the jailing of two Mexicans," she told him. "Last night, a couple of Mexicans jumped off the train and they hadn't eaten in days and when they came to Miller's pond, they found a swan egg and ate it."

"How the hell do you eat a swan egg?"

"You don't, really. You puncture a hole in the shell and drink it. There's lots of good nutrients, but it makes you sick afterward. Anyway, the female attacked, and one of the Mexicans used a pocketknife to ward her off, stabbed her to death. Miller had them arrested."

Vito shook his head in disbelief. "I can't believe those fucking border patrol assholes can just invade the camp like this and arrest anybody. Damn."

"They should have known they could have knocked on any door and we would have gladly fed them. But they were young and had probably been terrorized by Mexican gangs. They didn't trust anyone."

"Yep, that's the old Miller I know, that's his way of sending a message. Don't fuck with his property . . . like his son."

They arrived at the camp as dozens of geese descended on the fields. Some men were playing chess and dominos in the yards and women were clustered at picnic tables while others walked or stood in open spaces and talked. Chickens and goats scattered as they parked in front of the boxcar. Once inside, Vito paused in the doorway. Carmen pointed him to the chair at the table and reheated a pot of beans and chili. Vito sat for dinner at the table with his father. Carmen served them steaming bowls of rice and beans and excused herself, saying she had errands to run.

Vito watched her cross the compound toward the river, lingering at the hens. His eyes went from his father's immobile face and limp body to the now-rusting oil lamp that used to flicker in his mother's hand when she would check up on them at night.

The flame hovered, illuminating long-buried memories of his father—his foamy jaw as he shaved with a barber's razor, tinkering with the ironing board, embering the woodstove at dawn, retelling a worker's story of escaping from ICE with such animation that he made listeners believe it was a greater miracle than the parting of waters in the Bible, at the table with a cup of coffee warming his palms, listening to Mexican music, looking out the screen door at someone walking past and seeing something in the person that made his father's eyes go melancholy and his features somber and sad, a sadness with no words.

A wave of compassion for his father compelled him to rise and embrace him. With moistened eyes, he muttered hoarsely about how there had been many times he had disappointed his father's expectations but that there was no lack of love between them.

Casimiro wanted to question him, *Where have you been? You look very healthy. How is school going? How is Rafael? Did Miller give you permission to visit me?* Vito saw the desire to communicate in his father's eyes and reached over the table and held his hand, thought he felt it tense for a second.

He brushed his father's hair back, kissed his head. He adjusted a napkin under his chin, dragged a chair next to his, and sat and spooned him beans and rice, wiping the corners of his lips. It was an effort not to cry and rage at the injustice of it. After dinner, he pushed his father's wheelchair out and down the boxcar ramp, facing him toward the field. Vito sat on the ground next to him.

"Those chickens," he started, "I still blame them for distracting me." He looked at his hand with the scar on his pinkie. "You warned me not to mess with them. Many memories, Papa . . ." He stopped, afraid of the emotion mounting in him. He wiped his eyes and ended, "Ahh, what a nice life you gave us."

Casimiro commanded his eyes to speak, to respond, to magically make tongues appear in the air or to protrude from his sockets and string words together in a sentence, but even this desire withered, for his mind failed to order it. It infuriated him and his passion to fight it, to confront it, to overcome it resulted in gibberish grunts that enraged him.

"I saw Lorenzo. He's in El Paso doing business," Vito lied. "Mexico's thinking of getting into the chili business," he said, which was true, he'd heard it on the radio.

On the surface, his grim-lipped sullenness showed, but Casimiro smiled inside to himself. He knew the soul of the chili could never be reproduced in Mexico, not anywhere on the planet. It was about the spirit in the soil.

Vito sat in silence, absorbing the memories leaping from the elm tree with the clotheslines tied to its branches, the warehouse packing sheds, and the worn paths and roads leading to the fields, from where Carmen now came walking up in the dusk, carrying a stack of homemade tortillas wrapped in dish towels and a big bowl of menudo.

She was upset, her silence pulsed red; the heat of her eyes could boil water.

She went in and put the food away, pushed Casimiro inside, undressed him, dabbed his body with a warm washcloth, and laid him in bed. She kissed his forehead and signaled for Vito to follow her.

They leaned against the corral. He watched the horses as she casually pulled fresh grass and fed them. He dared not speak because she might be upset with something he had done. But that wasn't it.

She was thinking about the two Mexicans being arrested for eating the swan egg. There was absolutely no doubt in her mind. When a person is hungry and he can save his life by eating an egg, he has a right to that egg.

And it was not because they killed the swan, or ate the egg, no, the real reason they were put in jail and charged was that they had destroyed the fairy tale in the mind of the rich landowners— pond, swans, big house. It's the same old King Arthur and the holy grail bullshit. From the outside, life is beautiful and perfect, there's no injustice, no hunger, life is peaceful and nurturing.

Those two Mexicans shattered that fantasy and that's why they were put in jail, because in eating the egg they crushed the fable concealing the lie, she thought. Because the lie that comforted Miller, the lie he saw when he looked out his window and saw how peaceful and rich he was, how good life was, how everything and everyone was content and in its place and thriving—those Mexicans didn't kill a swan, they killed the lie that life was perfect.

"We should make some swan burritos, swan tacos." She said it to herself.

"What? What's the matter?"

"Nothing." She made kissing sounds and the horse came over. She patted his mane. She rubbed the horse's belly and scratched behind its ears, calmed herself by caressing the horse. The horse kept nudging her hand. "I know, baby, I know."

"How you talk to him is how I talked to you a hundred times, in my head," he admitted. "Just imaginary talks, you with me."

"It's called infatuation, Vito."

"You have to admit the first time we saw each other there was some strong chili sauce between us. Most people see cupids and arrows when they fall in love, I saw chili pies flying in my dreams."

She frowned, squinted, and nodded at him. "That's a lame attempt at flirting. We barely hung out a day or two. You're nuts, Vito. I love Lorenzo. Respect that or I'll bust your balls." She smiled. "Besides, what would those Budweiser girls in your hot tub think. And that day or two was enough to know that *every* woman is the apple in your eye."

"True, true."

They walked down the dirt road that cut between the fields. The air was heavy with coming rain, red and green chili peppers spicing the air. Lights glowed from houses and trailers, the river was quiet, poultry and goats nestled under porches and cars, and the only sound came from the packing sheds, where workers laughed as they oiled the conveyor belts and did monthly maintenance on the tractors.

"Over there," he pointed to an old elm tree, "Papa quartered two goats someone found on the highway shoulder. The female was pregnant and Papa pulled out two fetuses and after that I had the worst nightmares." He paused, studying her round-toe boots, the blue braid edging her jean hems, the curve of her legs and her nice, full hips. "By the way, you ever finish your dissertation?"

"Sure, with flying colors. I'm working on a book now about the migrant life." She looked into his eyes. "Lorenzo started hanging out with Felipe, going to Juárez, gambling at the casino, he got into using cocaine."

"Cocaine? Lorenzo? I thought maybe they busted him for weed. He wasn't dealing it, was he?"

"No, no, he would never do that. He used it, mostly just weekends. I tried it once, before we made love, and hated it. When he snorted it, I could tell the difference in him right away." She gazed at the fields. "It changed him. I think he even fucked around on me."

They walked.

Vito said, "I know a lot of good boxers that got fucked using that shit."

A soccer ball came bouncing toward him and Vito leaped and kicked it high and far and four kids chased after it across the field, illuminated by flashes of distant lightning.

"I warned them to stay inside but they don't believe lightning could hit them."

"No soccer kid with *corazón* would ever let lightning chase him off the field."

"The lights from the barracks over there, that's our schoolhouse. Tutors teach migrants English, computer skills, and GED. Lorenzo's money made that happen. There's also a physical therapist, the handicap van, the wheelchair, it cost over a hundred thousand, easy. Listen, coyotes in the distance."

She started talking again, filling him in on what had happened in the camp while he was gone.

"When your dad had the stroke we had to drive to Cruces, a good hour, all of us in the back of the truck. Lucia took his shoes and socks off and packed his feet and groin in ice. We took his clothes off and wiped him with a cold rag. Some of the women rubbed ice on his face. We forced him to drink water." She stopped walking.

They sat on a log next to the field, facing east. The moon gave enough light to see the fields. Crates and gunnysacks were piled and stacked next to cars and trucks that were parked alongside the field where the migrants left off picking.

"In the fight game there are just as many shattered dreams as there are in these fields . . . we just make a lot more money for the punishment we take."

"On weekends some of the men would go into town to a sports bar to see you on pay-per-view. In the ring in Vegas, mariachis serenading your entrance, flowers tossed as you walk— what kid wouldn't want that when you're as poor as they are. Becoming you is their goal in life."

"You win, you're loved; you lose, you're despised."

"When you left I started working with the migrants. I knew nothing about picking; interviewing them was one thing but I wanted to work with them. Your brother and I worked side by side and soon I picked as fast as anyone. But during those weeks and months I fell in love with him. At night we went out and rode horses, in the day we worked together, and before you knew it I couldn't go an hour without seeing him."

"Right there," he pointed to where four dirt roads met. "That's where I beat Miller's boy. Remember that, *whack, whack, whack!*" He threw a few jabs at the air and did a little dance. "I was moving dirt to build that dumb golf course; can you imagine, in the middle of the desert?"

Back at the camp a pack of kids emerged from the dark, shoving toward him. One pushed a black marker at Vito. "*Firme, firme, firme,*" he pleaded, while his friends lunged and pulled to get an autograph on their T-shirt, sneakers, notebook, arms, or hands, and then they dissolved into the dark.

She sighed and gave Vito a big hug. "Get some sleep. I'm happy you're home again."

"It's a whole new world."

"Good night. I'll meet you here four thirty." Carmen crossed the fields, going toward the river and the house she and Lorenzo shared.

40

How stunning the morning desert was to Vito. His heart burst with pleasure and a desire for his childhood days when the sun radiated one tiny ray of faith on his life, a ray that had weight, one he could toss from hand to hand and hold up and carry in his pocket and embrace before sleep and kiss at daybreak.

Fields steamed dew as the pickers arrived. Men, women, and children humped in the furrows, *picking*. Carmen slept the whole way. He was thinking bad thoughts as her chest rose and fell. He looked away, told himself to stop thinking of touching her. He told himself to shake it out of his head, he could control his mind, he was a trained boxer, he could discipline his body and mind, he could fuck any chick he wanted, but something else was pulling him.

In the miles that stretched out before them he wished Carmen wasn't engaged to his brother, that she was like so many he'd had—a free-loving chick who just wanted to fuck all night. But no, he was on a mission, and he would never betray his brother.

Still, he reached out and his fingers grazed her cheek and the sweetness of her sleeping face and her breath made something in his chest tighten.

He forced his mind to obey his will and pulled it back to what he was going to do—the upcoming fight—but her jeans were tighter at her crotch and the fine black hair on her arms and upper lip and between her eyebrows made his dick hard. He quit looking at her, determined to be strong and allow no thought of her body to fill his mind. He turned up the radio, shifted in his seat, and started thinking about the fight.

A few miles down the road he slowed for a roadblock. The solemn radiance of the desert morning convulsed suddenly into a military camp as armed National Guardsmen approached. They eyed him quickly, squinting into the passenger-side window at Carmen still asleep, waved him through, their eyes following him with suspicion.

Thirty minutes later, he saw a concrete building a few hundred yards from the freeway and he guessed there were at least four hundred people standing behind the barbed-wire fence that encircled a big, dirt yard. A gun tower stood at each of the corners. A large sign facing the freeway read HUTTO PRISON.

He felt queasy. The prisoners stared at him as he drove slowly past tanks and soldiers and laser-beam monitoring machines and sound and motion sensors. Some of the women, children, and men were confined in chicken-wire cages. Others were milling around in a larger cyclone-fence enclosure. A few more, a dozen or so, had their backs turned to him and were lined up against a wood fence.

He guessed it was some kind of temporary holding facility for Mexicans caught crossing the border illegally but it looked too much like a military war encampment with the jeeps, armed guards, military personnel, and white trailer offices. It scared him.

He watched as a canvas-covered Army jeep pulled into the encampment and was inspected by the guards at the gate, which was swung open by guard-tower sentries and allowed to enter and park. He watched as inmates of all ages—the men all handcuffed—were led out of the back of the truck and escorted into a separate fence yard.

What the hell is going on, he wondered as an ICE helicopter shattered his thoughts, patrolling overhead. Then it flew off, trailing armed guards in a machine-gun jeep that drove out to the desert.

Once he passed the Army operations base, he locked cruise control at eighty, lowered his window, and relaxed. Twenty minutes later a group of Mexicans rose like roadside ghosts in the shimmering heat. Beyond the road shoulder, dehydrated and clearly in need of medical attention, they pled for him to stop. He kept driving, not daring to look back in the rearview mirror. He was afraid.

41

They arrived in San Diego on Thursday night, eight hours after they had left Las Cruces. Carmen was delighted to be there, energetic and revived. She directed him through middle-class Mexican neighborhoods for a half hour until they pulled up to a rundown bungalow rental in the university area.

She invited Vito in, adding that her friends were throwing a big party and he better come, but he needed to get a motel room and rest, take a nap, then go to the storage facility nearby and load up all the belongings she wanted to take with her. He'd be back later.

When he returned hours later, the party was well underway. College kids came and went and girls danced on the porch and lawn to blaring music.

Carmen was already high on life and giggly on pot when he arrived. She had a lot of friends and the house was packed shoulder to shoulder, everyone hip bumping to the music and talking loud. He gulped down the first mixed drink offered and lost count after that. He was having a lot of fun telling stories of his life on the road as a boxer and the women surrounded him three deep.

They were party girls, carefree and smiling with no idea how the night was going to turn out, smiling with the expectation that it was going to be a lovely evening. And it was. People gathered around the barbecue laughing and eating, girls ran from guys, couples jumped in the pool and wrestled. The music was oldies but goodies, the weather was perfect and balmy.

Late at night the party started to dwindle, and after a while there were only six or seven people left, smoking weed and philosophizing.

He didn't remember how he and Carmen were left alone. They said good night to everyone leaving and the hostess went to her bedroom with some guy. He and Carmen were sitting on the couch—the room and the house were mellow, the lights amber and shaded low, Van Morrison on the stereo.

One of Carmen's girlfriends saw them fucking on the rug but Carmen was oblivious to the world. She was in a totally different zone and her mind was not fully conscious of what she was doing or the consequences of it, her body was feeling such intense pleasure, such sheer joy and lust in fucking.

Her friend's house with the windows illuminated by street lights, the bawdy voice of Morrison, the sultry moist ocean air, the wine and the weed and Vito's strong hands and firm body, all combined to create an erotic weight that pressed in on her from all sides and kept her down on her back with Vito on top of her as she whirled into an oblivious meltdown of dizzying joy.

For that twenty minutes she had him.

Then something blew inside of her, crossed from outside to inside and swept through her with a cold embracing chill, telling her she knew what she was doing, telling her she was lapping the kill's warm blood, filling her with the knowledge that she'd never give up those twenty minutes of her life and that she'd sacrifice everything for those minutes with him, and she grieved that she did.

That twenty minutes was her twenty and she had control of everything.

42

They left San Diego at dawn, her belongings in the back of the truck and covered with a tarp, and they hit open prairie after an hour, her eyes closed in self-disgust. Everything she looked at reflected her self-loathing. Behind her eyelids she smelled her unwashed hair. She scratched one bare foot with the other, wiping dirt off her soles with her toenails. Some things you could wipe off; others leave an indelible stain.

Her silence made him anxious so he told her he had seen the National Guard erecting electric fences, laying sensor-detection cable, that there were aerial drones following above.

He mentioned seeing the prisoners waving at him on the drive to San Diego, that he had kept on driving. He threw in that he didn't think it was right to cross without a legal permit. People crossing over in the thousands created chaos.

He should have woken her, he should have stopped for them, she grumbled.

What about his parents? she asked accusingly.

It was a different time and circumstance, he countered sharply.

She was pissed off and there wasn't much to say—he sensed her temper had deeper levels, a long white trail of fiery debris.

Her big brown eyes settled on him, studying his face.

He shuddered under the heaviness of his betrayals—
Lorenzo, still awaiting his bail hearing in jail, and the Mexicans he just drove by.

She swallowed hard. She felt like she might burst out weeping. She looked away, drowning in her own confusion and the
guilt that filled hundreds of prairie miles, extending all the way
to the horizon.

Vito was lost in his own thoughts as they drew ever closer,
with every mile, to his brother's eyes.

He wanted to blurt out, scream and slam the dashboard with
his fist, that it hadn't happened, that someone put some kind of
drug in his drink, that it was her fault, that something evil had
possessed them, someone had slipped them a poison and that was,
that was, that was . . . but it wasn't why.

He saw the outline of the mountains behind the town and
knew that within an hour he'd be standing in front of his brother.
Lorenzo had said he would make bail and meet them at the camp.
Vito was afraid to call and confirm that he was already there.
Lorenzo was certain to notice the tremor in his voice. Numbed
with fear and grief over doing this to his brother, Vito gripped
the wheel and stared ahead seeing nothing but what he had done.

Would he shoot him, beat her, move away, never come
back, never see him again? He drove on with an urge to yank
the wheel hard, right into one of the oncoming tractor trailers
roaring past, one behind another, from the opposite direction.
His eyes locked on Carmen's, asking for help, for reasons, for
anything that would alleviate his regret.

It could have been five minutes or five hours. The sky was darkening, sunlight spreading across the familiar landscape of the workers' trucks and cars parked alongside the fields while the workers were huddled together in the rows.

He pulled off the highway and turned west, down a long slope toward the river and the camp. Then he turned right, down a long row with trees on the left, thick and green running parallel to the road. Kids fished, women visited on porches, dogs chased his bumper. Normal images, and yet the world as he knew it had shattered into a million pieces.

He turned right, then left, into an open clearing, going past the boxcar and their house and other one-room homes, and bearing off to the left, scattering chickens, goats, and dogs, finally parking in front of the barn where he could see women boxing chili.

Lorenzo appeared framed in the doorway like a hero in a cowboy movie, shining and compassionate, smiling with extended arms wide in a mock embrace, elated.

He dashed out, slammed the hood of the truck with the palm of his hand, woke Carmen up, and swung her door open. She leaped out of the cab, rushed him and kissed him, weeping.

And as Lorenzo hugged her, laughing and asking why she was crying, he looked over her shoulder at Vito, sitting, unable to move or smile.

43

November 2008

A few months later, after endless nights of insomnia, agony, and sullen brooding, he was jogging alongside a field when he saw Lorenzo standing among a group of workers. He asked Lorenzo to walk with him while he cooled down.

As Vito stretched on the ditch bank, Lorenzo said, "In five months, after the title shot, we'll have the money we need to buy that section and build our homes. I've been up at night figuring it out, we need around another hundred and fifty thousand. Man, it's going to be nice, long time coming." He slapped Vito on the back and rubbed his palms together.

Vito stood up and announced he was leaving.

Lorenzo tossed a pebble at Vito and said, "Don't fuck around." He skipped a rock over the ditch water.

"I'm *serious*," Vito said. "HBO wants to film me, right up to fight night."

Lorenzo turned to face his brother. "What? What'd you say?"

"Gotta go to L.A."

"That's a joke, right? I'm your manager. Rafael is moving here to train you, what do you mean?"

"They're doing a documentary and I gotta be there."

Lorenzo said, "No, no, no, you're losing me here, little brother. Level with me."

"I have to leave . . . in the morning . . . I have to work things out."

"What the fuck do you mean work things out? I'm here for you, no matter what it is."

Carmen was coming up the ditch. She was showing.

Vito said, "It'll be good for us in the end, more money, then you can step back in to fill the shoes, but for now, I have to go with Luis and Bobby as my trainer and manager. I'm going to get a couple more miles."

Lorenzo watched him jog off.

"You're shaking." Carmen touched his arm.

"Vito's going to L.A. HBO's doing a documentary on him." Lorenzo stared after Vito in disbelief.

"It'll be okay."

"What?" Lorenzo turned, distracted. "What?"

That evening Lorenzo sat on the corral fence and watched Vito load his bags into his truck. Rage pounded his heart so hard he could feel a throbbing in his fingertips.

I shouldn't have been surprised, he said to himself, then thought, *he's always fucked things up and he's doing it again.*

But Lorenzo sensed there was something else compelling his brother's departure. He saw it then, and saw it again the next day—something unsettling in Vito's eyes when he backed his truck out and swung it around and paused ever so briefly before driving away.

"Don't call, or come back . . . ever," Lorenzo said and climbed between the corral posts toward his horse.

44

December 2008

From the moment he rented the small room above Topo's Club-house in East L.A., then later on the bench where he changed into his black shorts, high-top sneakers, and tank top in the locker room, he was all about his shot at the title—furiously disman-tling sparring partners with a beat-down, no-holds, bring it on attitude. His manager, Miguel "Lucky" Fuegos, and the Filipino trainer, Negreton "Neto" Chavez, had to back him off his op-ponents, rein him in. It was this way for over two months, until late January.

   Vito trained with fierce determination, showing up on time each day, putting in his ten hours, urged on by Neto's constant compliments, displaying magnificent defense skills, hand speed, and brilliant offense. Vito would stay late to watch reel upon reel of his opponents' fights, scrutinizing each round, stopping the reel, nodding to himself, rewinding, and forwarding again and again with infinite patience. And over time, Neto admitted that he had never witnessed such mastery of the ring, such quick reflexes, such ability to counter his opponent's punches with dazzling accuracy and, over time, to draw standing-room-only crowds to enjoy the spectacle. It was as if someone had programmed Vito. And still he plunged into the public's adoration and gave them back every bit of attention they desired.

People enjoyed his antics, which were always fresh and inventive. And spectacle that it was, he would laugh with the people, often playfully boxing with a spectator and pretending when the spectator hit him that it was a solid, knock-out smack, and like a Charlie Chaplin, he'd wobble around the ring, falling and getting up. Or, embracing two women, one in each arm, he would dance the polka in the ring as the crowd whistled and clapped and hollered with pleasure.

He belonged to them, was their hero and rebel, shield of honor and symbol of strength—the very soul of the culture, a *corazón de la gente*. Vito came out of nowhere, a great fighter, and he beat down every opponent of every color. And he enjoyed their tribute and adoration. At Cigaro's cantina, where he went to eat dinner, Cigaro had a corner booth for Vito, and no one but Vito and his guests could sit in it. He would sit like a king as people stopped to tell him how much they loved and respected him.

Then, for no reason, on a fine, brisk morning he was a no-show for his regular seven-mile jog. Neto waited for an hour, called Vito on his cell, and then drove to the Clubhouse. He was pissed. Before taking Vito on, he had warned that he wouldn't tolerate bullshit, this was a serious game. He had his reputation at stake.

Over time, it got worse and though Neto didn't want to admit it, Vito was too good, too gifted, too beautiful a fighter, so after torrential curses, he chased Vito down and forced him to train. And so it went—he trained him when he found him but most of the time Vito was nowhere to be found.

No matter how many times Neto and Lucky went down, cajoled, chided, and sweet-talked Vito to come to the gym and train, he refused. He was drinking more, a different woman draped his arm every night, and, more worrisome, he was hanging out with mafia characters, drug dealers, and shot callers.

Neto and Lucky gave up and took on other contenders, who would inevitably ask about Vito. They always responded with a discouraging shake of the head.

It was the sight of the man at the bar that had spun Vito off-kilter.

He was drunk the night he first saw him and because he couldn't be sure it was the same man, he returned to the bar nightly, in hopes of seeing him again. Vito called his brother but Lorenzo cut him off, telling him not to call, and hung up. His brother's condemnations sent him out into the night, drinking at clubs, challenging anyone who dared give him a look or get in his way.

One thing never changed, though, and no matter where he was, how late it was, going home or to a party, Vito always made time to stop in at the bar and nurse a few drinks, waiting for the man to appear again.

The man didn't show for weeks. Then, on a Friday night, Vito was one of three patrons still in the bar drinking. Around three in the morning he rose to leave, unsteady, leaning on the table, and when he turned toward the door, the man was there.

Their eyes locked and each scrutinized the other. He was lean and gaunt-faced, dressed in black boots, jeans, a shirt, and a red vest. His belt, boot tips, and heels were adorned with buffalo nickels and strapped to his left hip was a bowie knife with a nickel-plated handle.

Vito had to grab the bar counter to keep from murdering the man. The room spun, cold sweat poured down his face, chest, and armpits, and his heart pounded as if two bobcats were thrashing in his ribcage. Something stuck in his throat. He reached for his cell, fingers trembling so severely he could barely punch the numbers. When his brother's recorded voice answered, Vito whispered hoarsely, "I found him, Lorenzo, the one who killed Mom." He dropped his cell phone, picked it up, and looked around.

The man was gone.

Vito ran for the back door. He looked frantically in one direction and then the other. There were only bums and derelicts sharing wine, huddled in their smelly rags for the night in their cardboard boxes and threadbare blankets over by Dumpsters.

His cell phone rang. At first there was a long silence but then he heard Lorenzo's voice saying, "Are you sure?"

"I'm sure. I never forgot those buffalo-nickel boots. All my life they've been in my dreams."

"Where you at?"

45

Here is what happened that night in the alley behind the cantina.

He said it was as wrong as not having horses on earth, or a planet absent of wind, moon, and sun. I dragged on my cigarette and turned to the voice speaking and saw the man from the train many years ago.

Anywhere, he went on, but not there, not there, he said, pointing to his groin. I flicked my cigarette, mashed it with my high heel and moved to go inside but his hand gripped my shoulder and stopped me.

I had felt that grip before. I turned and smiled and asked, Why did you try to rape me? Who are you, really? You said you were from Culiacán and smiled at me.

He screamed, You do not stab a man there! It is against life itself, a crime against humanity!

And what about raping a sixteen-year-old virgin? Is that not against humanity?

He pinned me against the wall and unsheathed his nickel-plated bowie knife and held it under my chin.

I smelled his cigarettes and whiskey breath; his flesh felt wild, as if it had been warmed only by campfires.

There was such a sadness in the fist that clenched my hair and such horrible adolescent hurt in the chest that pushed my body against the wall, and his face, oh my God, his face—unshaven, with thin lips and thin eyebrows, the yellow teeth—I sensed how much horror he had suffered.

I took a full breath in and felt the blade cut through my skin, then against bone.

In that moment I cared about all life, grieving as I let go—made of bamboo, my soul was sand and I was turned upside down and I heard the cussshhhh *of my soul-sand returning to the earth, dust to dust.*

46

Vito didn't sleep that night, or the next. Circles darkened his eyes. His entire life now narrowed to this sharp hour, this target: Buffalo Nickel man. Memories rippled out from the source of all pain. Vito felt like a child again. His eyes widened as large as the black sky, filling his soul with a tormenting rain of sadness that never stopped. He wept, pacing back and forth in his room, crying for the four-year-old crawling on the floor as his brother chased him under tables and around the legs of patrons who watched Nopal's two kids invent silly games. That's where he was when he saw the nickel boot tips and heels, heard the *click-click* sound they made on the hardwood floor as they passed him— and since then, passing a thousand times in his sleep.

Driving the southern route from Cruces to Tucson, the beauty of the moon cooled Lorenzo's rage. Leaving Yuma, the sun rising over the desert took his breath away. He pulled over and parked and something felt like it snapped in him and he sat on the ground, leaning against the right rear fender and again, he wept.

He drove on with a fierce willfulness, his mind fixed on the business ahead.

He arrived in East L.A. the next day, late in the afternoon, went directly to Vito's apartment, pulled up, and found Vito sitting outside on the steps. He looked bad. Vito walked up the walkway and opened the truck door and hugged Lorenzo and Lorenzo embraced him back.

"Take me up to your place. You gotta wash, you stink. I'll make some coffee."

Vito paused at the entrance.

"Come on, it'll be okay," Lorenzo assured him.

That night they hung out at the bar until closing and just as Vito said, the man appeared. Lorenzo saw the man's nickel-tipped boots and nickel-plated heels and they were the same ones he'd seen as a kid at the bar where his mother sang.

Lorenzo told Vito to stay put and nurse his beer while he took a stool at the counter next to the man. He started up a casual conversation, about how coming in late was a good time to pick up women because that was when they were drunk and ready for bedding, but the man knocked back his tequila shot and headed for the back exit.

Lorenzo followed and Vito came up after him.

The man was out back smoking, leaning against the wall, one leg crooked. He turned to the brothers and his eyes squinted at them and he reached for the bowie knife at his belt.

Vito sprang and kicked the knife away, punching him repeatedly and without mercy. Jaw bone cracked. Ribs broke. Nose was smashed. Cheek bones shattered. And then there was his brother coming at the man from behind, wielding the bowie knife in his hand. As if in a slow-motion nightmare, Lorenzo slid the blade across the man's Adam's apple and whispered, "This is for our mother!"

Vito staggered in horror as the man slumped to the ground, blood squirting from his neck. Lorenzo knelt beside the man, shook the man's head, and yelled, "Understand me? You had this coming. Tonight is the night of understanding, muthafucker!"

The man gave a muffled groan as Lorenzo shoved the man's face into the pool of blood until he quit breathing.

Sirens closed in from a distance and Lorenzo ordered Vito to run but he refused.

"I'm with you."

Lorenzo grabbed his brother and threw him against the wall and cried out, "You leave! Now! You get you ass in gear and train hard, win that title, for our mom and dad! You understand me? You understand . . ."

"Yes."

"Go. Everything will be fine, champ. And get Rafael down here to train you again."

The cops arrived and arrested Lorenzo. Vito walked on the sidewalk, an anonymous pedestrian in the crowd. Lorenzo spent the drive to the police station in the backseat, handcuffed and bloody. Vito glanced at him as he passed and they both nodded, knowing they had done what had to be done.

47

March 2009

The big title fight was a week away and Rafa was pushing Vito hard. He wanted him to be in top condition. They were now coming back from a fifteen-mile run in the steep hills near Santa Barbara.

Rafa drove and Vito was sitting shotgun in the truck, half dozing and half remembering his earlier days fighting in small village rodeos on New Mexico ranches where a couple of cowboys flagged you in between two tall pine trees with a sign nailed to the bark that read THE FIGHT.

Rafa asked, "You hear who's back? Harold's little brother, Cobra, ranked top ten now. He'll be gunning for you soon."

Vito stirred awake, selected songs on his iPod, and slipped his earphones on. He unwrapped a candy bar and munched, nodding to the music. Rafael reached over and unplugged the wire. He repeated the information and then said, "Hope you're ready."

"Hope so, too." Vito liked to irritate Rafael with modest affection. "When he's not fighting, he's chained to his daddy's tractor hitch, plowing up field boulders."

"I think he lives around here, one of these little towns."

"And you think I'm all goose down and swan fluff?" Vito continued trying to provoke him, but Rafael didn't fall for it. "All I said was he's ranked and tough."

And as the truck jumbled down the dirt road to the farm house, Ignacio, who was sleeping in the middle between them, woke up and yawned. "We here?" he asked, and rubbed his eyes.

Vito opened the truck door and stood on the running board. He jumped off and yelled back to Rafa, "I'll meet you there." They still had two hours of sparring to do in the barn, which they had outfitted with a ring and body and speed bags.

Months ago, when Vito had visited his brother in the L.A. county jail, Lorenzo told him to rent a farm outside of Santa Barbara and set up a training facility. And since the place had lush acres of rolling sweet grass, Lorenzo had Vito buying livestock to start herds back home someday—cows, bulls, horses, and sheep.

Now, Vito walked over to a holding pen to check out a new batch of Texas longhorns fresh from the auction. "Boy, you got balls big as a trucker's ass," he spit at the steer's head, hitting it right between the eyes on its big bony forehead. "And you," he said, walking over to a white-faced cow, "are as cute as a girl-friend I once had."

The fight was to be held at the Staples Center in Los Angeles and promoters had billed it as the biggest clash between two heavy-weight titans since the thriller from Manila, with Muhammad Ali and Joe Frazier. Bobby "Warlock" Malone, the undefeated world champion from England, against Vito "Fieldworker" Lucero, also known as the man with the magic carpet ride because he had ascended the ranks so fast.

That evening a sell-out crowd squeezed into the arena, more people than Vito had ever imagined might come to see him fight—millionaires and Hollywood stars thirty deep at ringside, and all the way up near the rafters were the rag-footed, scrub-jean workers.

Snapping his jabs and storming pure destruction through his punches, Vito warmed up in the locker room, smashing the body bag until he was sweating and in the humming trance of a warrior on a religious mission.

He didn't see anyone anymore, didn't notice the girls flirting with him or the men that wanted him beat down like a dog, nor did he think about the money—Warlock, his opponent, filled him with rage, a blistering rage, a blinding hot-flash rage, he was the emissary of all landowners, the representative of all evil.

He put on the kid's gloves, which he hadn't worn for a long time, the ones he had found in the trunk of the car long ago, and after Rafael laced them up, he kissed them, knelt, and prayed. Then he rose, uncharacteristically quiet and somber, thinking of his family, the fields, his father and brother and mother and the life he used to have.

"It's worse than I thought," Rafael said, worry etched in his face. Vito said nothing. "You're fighting the dirtiest fighter there is."

Vito spit, "Good, good." Vito was in a zone that Rafael had never seen him in before a fight. It was the first fight where Vito didn't take the mic and cajole the crowd. He looked at Rafa and asked, "Is tonight Good Friday?"

"I don't think so, is it?" He looked at Ignacio, who didn't know—he hadn't attended church in twenty years.

"Someone's got to pay for Christ's suffering on the cross." They all smiled.

They entered the arena, mariachi music blaring until Vito was in the ring. A cheer went up; the Chicanos and Mexicans were expecting Vito to say something but he remained quiet and that disturbed them, especially after the announcer introduced Warlock and a riotous clamor went up. "*War-lock! War-lock! War-Lock!*"

Vito studied his beefy opponent and muttered, "A clubhouse prince I am going demote down to backdoor toss, to dog's butcher scraps." Warlock's mashed nose looked like the end of a drill bit. He sported a mustache and sideburns, and his trunks bore the image of a Warlock with mountain goat horns and a sword. The flesh around his eyes was permanently swollen from too many punches. The gauzy illumination of the rafter lights cut at his features, making him appear shadowy and menacing.

The bell rang and Vito sprinted out, dancing on his toes, smacking Warlock with quick jabs, slicing at him, kidneys, ribs, arms, mocking as Warlock counterpunched but hit only air.

Vito snapped quick stinging rights at Warlock's face and midsection at will but Warlock managed to land a punch on Vito's face, causing his eyes to burn and tear up, blurring his vision. After a while there was nothing Vito could do but tie him up and battle inside, close up.

And that was what Warlock wanted.

He bit Vito on the shoulder. In another bear hug he slugged Vito's crotch and made him double over in pain while he beat Vito from behind. Vito was losing, and the more he pounded inside, retaliating for every blow given, the more Warlock devastated him with crushing blows to the back, head, and ribs.

Round after round, Warlock was too big, pounding Vito with his enormous arms and legs, the layers of muscle under inches of skin and thick-boned joints were impervious. Vito's blows hardly fazed or slowed Warlock's pounding until Vito whispered something about how he knew Warlock's mother and the reason he couldn't hit him hard was because Warlock might be his own son—his mother worked the corner, giving it up for a suck on the crack pipe.

That was it.

Warlock went berserk, he tried to kick Vito, then lowered his head and shoulders and rammed Vito down to the canvas and bludgeoned him mercilessly with his fist and elbows, cracking his forehead against Vito's and opening a gash along the hairline.

The ref could do nothing and the fans screamed for blood. It was no longer a heavyweight title fight, but a barroom brawl.

Mumbled whispers of defeat rippled through the crowd and Chicanos grumbled louder and louder about Warlock cheating.

The casino owners and rich mobsters ringside were smiling, content that justice was being meted out in good old-fashion whiteboy ways. Warlock was going to win in any way at any cost.

Fans shouted to stop the fight. Others made their way through the crowd, got as close to ringside as they could, and cried for Vito to respond.

Rafa slapped his hands together yelling at Vito to get up. Between Warlock's flurry of blows, Vito glimpsed Rafa's face. He looked around and other faces reflected the fight's outcome—the expressions were disappointed and sullen, all thinking he was another wannabe champ who had raised their expectations but was now proving he didn't have the heart.

The crowd roared, *"Dale en la madre cabrón!* Put the son of a bitch down."

There were no more rounds or ref or judges, it was blood and sheer violence.

Warlock lunged with all his weight behind the punch into Vito's ribs and Vito buckled, cringed in agony, his heels kicking the floor he was in so much pain.

Shaking it off, Vito squirmed free of Warlock's armlock. Breathing and coughing, gasping for air, he danced and hopped and backpedaled around until he recovered his balance and the dizziness left his head.

Blood poured from the cuts on his head and mouth but it didn't stop him from mouthing off again.

"You be lucky if you're riding rims when I get done. You ever walk into L.A. traffic at rush hour? You're about to be under

the wheels buddy." Vito smiled, puffing, teeth red, blood oozing from his grin.

Lefts and rights, cuts and chops. Warlock panted, his face
looked like a twenty-car pileup and Vito was the tornado that
swirled around him. Warlock was spent, couldn't hold his arms
up, tried swinging but flailed haplessly. He had expended all his
energy trying for a quick knockout.

The momentum shifted and the crowd booed as Vito
slapped, played, then obliterated Warlock with fierce roundhouse
punches. Warlock's face went into Vito's gloves whole and came
out crushed, diced, and juiced. Then, as one of the grand sym-
bolic moves of the fight that was to be remembered for a long
time, to punctuate his dominance, Vito pushed Warlock through
the ropes, leaped over, and shoved him into the crowd, where
Warlock collapsed, blood bubbling from his nose and mouth and
every part of his face. Suddenly, Vito yelled at the audience, "My
brother is innocent!"

The fight was over. Warlock was slumped over and Vito
was in another world, even as the cops were called in and the
fans roared. Vito stared at the spectators and then rushed back to
the ring, grabbed the mic from the judge's table, and jumped up
to address the crowd.

"My brother is innocent," he repeated and, even as fans were
fighting the riot police near the entrances, he continued. "He's
in jail now, accused of murder, and he didn't do it. I did! In self-
defense, and now they're trying to pin it on my brother. The
man attacked me with a knife."

The crowd quieted. "I defended myself. Don't let injustice rule this land. This is America, where justice can prevail."

The giant crowd of Chicanos reeled as the flashy fight fans at ringside started making their way out, shouldering through the masses.

Vito ordered, "No, no, don't leave. We're in this together and we will make this country live up to its dream, the American dream!"

The crowd started chanting, "American dream! American dream!"

"I promise you, we will get there!"

In the roar of the crowd, even the judges and society's most upstanding members, sitting together in one section, gave almost imperceptible nods of assent and turned to leave.

"Thank you, thank you." Vito turned to the crowd. He slapped Ignacio's arm and delighted the crowd with fancy footwork dancing.

Mariachis followed him and swung into a vibrant polka song. People clapped and danced, doors swung open and the smoggy but beautiful air of Los Angeles filled the coliseum. Rafael shook his head in astonishment. He knew the heavyweight title had just gone out the window and that Vito would be put on a minimum one-year suspension and probably five years probation. But in a way, Rafael was okay with it—the world knew Vito was the champion, whether he wore the belt or not, and that suited Rafael just fine. He grabbed Vito to get him out before the cops put him in jail for inciting a riot.

48

Lorenzo watched the whole thing from his jail cell with mixed feelings. He wanted his little brother to win right, win clean, but he was glad he had defended himself and didn't let Warlock brutalize him. He knew Vito had the public behind him now. Vito was smart, and Lorenzo knew that was why he had done it. Public opinion counted a lot when it came to high-profile trials.

Three months later, when the trial began, such a large crowd arrived that reserve police were called in to monitor the mob. It was almost like a holiday—thousands and thousands of boxing fans showed up for Lorenzo's day in court. They barbecued on tailgates, brandished Mexican flags, and blasted *ranchera* music, gathering to still talk about the fight. Vito was their hero and to sweeten their adoration and loyalty to him, the day Lorenzo was declared innocent by virtue of self-defense, it seemed every single Mexican and Chicano in the world descended on Los Angeles. Freeways were packed, Los Angeles cantinas and restaurants were congested, the beach swarmed with kids and families and picnickers, and every hour radio stations announced the verdict and played celebratory music.

On a warm January morning, in 2009, Vito and Lorenzo left Los Angles and when they arrived back at the camp, Miller was true to his word and sold them the acreage next to his fields.

On May 14, 2009, after they had finished building two houses on opposite ends of the farm, they signed the papers to start their own agricultural chili business.

It was a Monday morning and Vito and Lorenzo were in the fields, working alongside the other field-workers, when Carmen came outside, holding her cell phone out to Vito and motioning that it was a call for him. Vito took the phone and walked away to talk in private.

She also had a bottle filled with ice-cold water that she handed to Lorenzo. He uncapped it and gulped heartily. Carmen unhitched the straps of her baby pack, set it on the ground, and lifted out their three-month-old daughter, Liliana.

Lorenzo took the baby in his arms and sat on the ground cradling her. He set her down in the dirt and sifted soil over her tiny hands. She cooed with pleasure.

Vito finished his call, knelt down next to Liliana, and looked up at Lorenzo, who said, "I know brother, I know. Isn't she beautiful?" He looked around the fields and at his house and his eyes settled on Carmen, then his brother.

Vito wondered what his brother meant by, "I know, brother, I know," but instead of asking he said, "That was the doctor, about my checkup last week."

"Everything okay?"

"You remember that arrowhead Mom put into my chest? When I was a baby?"

Lorenzo nodded and handed him the bottle of water.

Vito drank and said, "I got two choices. The doctor says if I want to box, he has to take it out. It's moved in, and he says if I got hit hard, it could puncture one of my vital organs. I think he meant my heart. Take it out and box or leave it in and never box again."

"What'd you decide?"

"It's part of mom. She stays with me."

Lorenzo handed Liliana to Carmen and patted his brother's shoulder. "Let's get this field done."

I'll never forget how, one night, with my two sons, I went to the river. Near the bank, in front of a cottonwood tree I called my tree. I undressed and danced and fell on the ground squirming and swiveling as if I was mating with the Earth.

I held the hands of my sons and crouched on the muddy bank and I dipped my hand in the water and wet our faces. I dried us off with my skirt and we laid back and while looking up at the night sky, I suddenly started crying. I yearned for Mexico.

I am crossing back now, a rare songbird, vanishing into the jungle. A bird without a name, that will appear to you only during certain times of the seasons.